A FAMILY AFFAIR

The Great War brings sadness for Nurse Emma Meadows and her parents: her brother has an accident while learning to fly a biplane, and after a neighbour spurns her, their young sister runs away from home. Emma, herself, loves Dr James Townsend and when he is reported dead on active service in France she goes there to learn the truth of his death — little knowing what she will find when she gets there.

CATRIONA McCUAIG

◆

A FAMILY
AFFAIR

Complete and Unabridged

LINFORD
Leicester

First published in Great Britain in 2010

First Linford Edition
published 2011

British Library CIP Data

McCuaig, Catriona.
  A family affair. - -
  (Linford romance library)
  1. Nurses- -Fiction. 2. World War,
  1914 – 1918- -Social aspects- -Fiction.
  3. World War, 1914 – 1918- -Casualties- -
  France- -Fiction. 4. Love stories.
  5. Large type books.
  I. Title II. Series
  823.9'2–dc22

  ISBN 978–1–4448–0893–3

Published by
F. A. Thorpe (Publishing)
Anstey, Leicestershire
Set by Words & Graphics Ltd.
Anstey, Leicestershire
Printed and bound in Great Britain by
T. J. International Ltd., Padstow, Cornwall

This book is printed on acid-free paper

1

Rose Meadows was alarmed to find her husband standing by the window with his hands in his pockets, his shoulders slumped. *Not more bad news!* she thought, crossing the room to put her arms around him. Since the war had started, every day seemed to bring some fresh worry.

'What's the matter, love? You look all in.'

'Rose! I didn't hear you come in. Did you want me for something?'

'I asked if there's anything the matter, Will. You seem to have the weight of the world on your shoulders. Is there something wrong at the school?'

William Meadows was headmaster of the Hartscombe Village school and Rose knew that he took his duties very seriously.

He sighed. 'Two more old boys in today's casualty lists, Rose. That brings it to eleven now, all youngsters I taught as little scamps, taken from us before they've had a chance to live at all. All that bright hope, vanished for good. What's the point of it all, eh? Just you tell me that.'

'I know, love. It hardly bears thinking about. Look, you come and sit by the fire, and I'll go and put the kettle on.' Will allowed himself to be led to his favourite chair, his face creased into lines of grief.

'I wish there was something more I could do,' Rose told the dog, as she laid the tea tray. 'All I've got to offer is a cup of tea and a hug, and that won't put the Kaiser on the run, will it, boy?' Old Towser thumped his tail.

Her husband was looking a bit more cheerful when Rose returned with his tea and biscuits. 'Thanks, love. I could do with this. Sorry if I sounded a bit downhearted a minute ago. Things were a bit fraught at school today, with young Miss Landers in tears because she has one of the dead lads' brothers in her class, and Miss Fiske muttering about how she'd love to get just five minutes alone with Kaiser Bill!'

Rose had to laugh. The thought of prim, grey-haired Miss Fiske facing up to the king's militant cousin was amusing, to say the least. 'Never mind. Surely this beastly war can't go on much longer, can it? Everyone said it would be over by Christmas, and that was almost a year ago!'

'I hope you're right, love, I hope you're right. I know it's selfish to think of our own family, when other parents have lost their own boys, but I hope and pray it ends before our children are called upon to take part.'

'No danger of that, I shouldn't think. Pierce is just a boy at the grammar school, and the girls are safe enough, Emma doing her nursing training, and Lucy here at home.'

Will patted his wife's hand. Rose needed protecting too, he thought.

Here in the peaceful Gloucestershire countryside it was hard to believe that a terrible war was waging on the other side of the English channel. It was here that his three children had been born, and here that he had seen them growing into chubby children, taking their first steps.

'Have you heard anything from Emma lately?' he asked, holding out his cup for a refill.

'Not since the letter that came last week. I showed you that, of course.'

'Funny she hasn't written since, then.'

'She's busier than ever, what with working twelve hours a day on the wards, and trying to study for final exams in her time off. And as if that isn't enough, they're all making dressings to send to the front — in their spare time, as Emma puts it!'

'Lucy seems very keen on going to those Red Cross meetings with you, love; rolling bandages and all that. I wonder if she'll follow in Emma's footsteps and go into nursing?'

Rose shook her head. 'For goodness' sake don't you go putting ideas like that into the child's head!'

'I don't see why not. It's a worthwhile career, and the knowledge will come in handy when she marries and has children of her own.'

'You know why not, Will Meadows, and I won't hear another word about it!' She quickly jumped up to her feet and began to pace around the room.

'That was years ago, love, when she was just a little thing, and according to old Doc Smart, she's fit as a fiddle now.'

'Pooh, what does he know about anything? He's behind the times, Will. If it wasn't for the fact that so many doctors have gone off to the war, he'd have been put out to pasture years ago.'

Will disagreed with his wife, but he held his peace. She was inclined to get upset when it came to talking about their Lucy's health. When she was little more than a toddler the child had been stricken with diphtheria, and for an agonising while it had seemed as if they might lose her. Strangely, the epidemic that had struck the district had passed both Emma and Pierce by. Apparently they had built up some sort of immunity to the disease, although nobody could explain how or why. Meanwhile, poor little Lucy had been taken to the fever hospital, much to her poor mother's distress because parents were not allowed to accompany their children there. The prevailing wisdom was that having visitors from home was not a good idea because the small patients became too upset when visiting hours were over, leaving the overworked nurses to deal with the tears and tantrums.

Will had never forgotten those anxious days when they'd waited in dread for word from the hospital. Finally little Lucy had come back to them, just a shadow of her former self. It had broken Rose's heart when the child had insisted on calling her 'Nurse' in her lisping voice, instead of Mummy. It was not surprising, then, that Rose had handled the little girl with kid gloves ever since.

Now, though, Lucy was blooming. Her rosy cheeks, sparkling eyes and shining hair all combined to make her a very pretty young girl, the picture of health. She had left school at fourteen and was now enjoying living at home with few responsibilities, other than joining her mother in such war work as came their way.

'I wonder where Pierce has got to?' Rose said suddenly. 'He should be home from school by now, wanting to know what's for tea, and how long it will be before he's called to the table! Honestly, Will, I don't know where that boy puts it all, and yet he's skinny as a rail!'

'He's been kept in, I shouldn't wonder, having to write lines. 'I must concentrate in class.' That sort of thing.'

'Surely not.'

'Actually, Rose, I've been meaning to

tell you. I had a visit from old Bruce the other day, my friend at the grammar school. He hummed and hawed a bit, and then he let slip that Pierce has fallen behind at school. He's been handing in shoddy work, or not completing homework assignments at all. To cut a long story short, the boy is failing badly, and unless he pulls up his socks he'll have no chance at all of getting into the university.'

'You'll need to give him a pep talk, then.'

'I'm afraid it's gone too far for that, love. No, we'll have to get him a tutor for weekends and holidays to give him some one-to-one instruction.'

Rose pulled a face. She'd never been too keen on book learning herself, and she could sympathise with her son.

'I know you'd like Pierce to follow in your footsteps, dear, but is it wise to push the lad? Perhaps he needs to be left to follow his own path.'

Will clicked his tongue in exasperation. 'It's my job as a father, never mind being a headmaster, to set an example to the boy. If I don't bring him into line, who will? I allow you to deal with the girls as you see fit; now you must let me handle my son in my own way. And just think on this, Rose,' he said, seeing that she was about to argue with him, 'If the boy is allowed to slack off, perhaps to the point where he drops out of school, where do you suppose that will lead? He'll be running off to join the army before we can turn around, and how would you like that?'

'Pierce is only seventeen.'

'Exactly. And next year he'll be eighteen.'

They were saved from any further discussion when the door flew open, revealing their youngest child, dressed in her oldest clothes.

'Hello, Dad! Did you have a good day? Mum, I'm just going down to the farm to help with the milking. All right?'

'But don't you want any tea, dear? I'll be dishing up as soon as Pierce gets in.

It's shepherd's pie, your favourite.'

'Oh, Aunt Lizzie will find me something, I expect. Can I go, then?'

'I suppose so, but don't be late back. The nights are getting cold, and I don't want you coming down with something nasty.'

'Don't worry, I'll run all the way. See you later!' Lucy disappeared, and moments later they heard the outer door slam.

2

At St Botolph's hospital, life went on much as usual on women's medical, the ward to which Emma Meadows had been newly assigned. In addition to her own duties, she had to keep an eye on Dorothy Trent, a young probationer who had recently come to join them.

'Dotty by name and dotty by nature,' Emma told her pal, Jenny, when they met in the queue in the dining hall during their tea break. 'Honestly, I want to help the girl, and I know that we made a few silly mistakes when we started out, but she takes the biscuit! Do know what she did yesterday? She only went off duty, leaving a kaolin poultice in the oven for Sister to find when it was practically burned to a crisp! And who do you think got the ticking off afterwards?'

'Talking of biscuits,' Jenny said, 'I was

hoping there might be one or two to have with our tea, but it doesn't look hopeful!'

'Doorsteps as usual,' Emma told her, craning her neck to see what was on the tables. 'Looks like jam, though, which is better than bread and scrape. Next time I go home I'll see if Mum has a pot of her homemade gooseberry to spare. I do love a nice jam sandwich.'

'I wouldn't if I were you. By the time you've offered it round the table there won't be much of it left. And you know we're not allowed to keep food in our rooms, worse luck! Are you coming to Red Cross tonight?'

Emma sighed. 'I suppose so, if I get off duty in time. Sister Martin is a stickler for every last job to be completed before we go. 'The night shift have enough to do, and I won't have it said that my nurses shirk their duties!' Honestly, Jenny, I'm beginning to dislike that woman. I thought Sister Gray was strict enough, but she wasn't a patch on old Martinet, as the others call her. Never mind. In a few months we'll be qualified, so at least we have that to look forward to.'

'I can't wait!' Jenny said.

'What will you do afterwards, go to France to nurse wounded soldiers?'

'Not much chance of that. They won't let you go until you're twenty-three. I fancy something where the discipline won't be quite so strict. Coming here was a shock to the system, I can tell you! I thought I could handle anything after boarding school, but I was wrong. Remember Sister Tutor sending me out of class because my hair had fallen out of its clasp?'

'You can laugh, Jenny Adams, but I hadn't been here two days when she pounced on me for showing too much ankle. She whipped out a ruler and measured the length of my skirt in front of the whole set. I had to spend the evening taking the hem down, instead of playing tennis with the rest of you!'

'It might be fun to be a matron or a sister tutor some day,' Jenny said

13

dreamily. 'I'd quite like to sit behind a desk, frowning on some poor shaking probationer who had broken a thermometer and come to confess.'

'You'd never last that long. You'll get married and have six children!'

'Chance would be a fine thing. Where are we supposed to meet men in this place? It's worse than a convent. Come on, Meadows, I spy two empty seats over there. We can sit together.' She rushed forward, earning a rebuke from the presiding sister, who reminded her that a nurse may only run in case of fire or hemorrhage.

★ ★ ★

The subject of marriage came up again when Emma was back on the ward, helping a patient with a steam inhalation. 'This will help your chest, Mrs Mack,' she said, as she draped a towel over the woman's sparse grey hair. The strong smell of friar's balsam wafted towards her.

When she returned later the patient emerged from under the towel, red-faced and dripping. 'Phew, it was hot under there, Nurse. Are you sure that stuff is doing me any good? I don't feel no better.'

'Give it time, Mrs Mack. You were so desperately ill when they brought you in that we can't expect a great improvement overnight. You really should have seen a doctor before things became this bad.'

'Doctors cost money, and I've got six kiddies to look after, with my Jack away in the army. You can't know what it's like, Nurse, you not being married, although I suppose you'll be getting wed one of these days?'

'I'm afraid not. Working the hours that we do there's no chance of meeting anyone; we're too tired to go out socially.'

'Go on with you! What about that nice doctor who comes to see me? A handsome bloke, he is, a real catch. I wouldn't have minded marrying him myself, except that nobody else could ever be as good as my Jack.'

Emma laughed. 'We're not allowed to speak to doctors, Mrs Mack. Not unless we want a quick trip to Matron's office to explain ourselves. Trainee nurses are supposed to know their place.'

The older woman's jaw sagged in disbelief. 'I never heard the like. What if he's wanted on that telephone contraption while him and that sister are standing here talking to me? Surely you can say something then?'

Emma shook her head. 'I'd have to address Sister, and she'd repeat the message to him.'

Mrs Mack's shoulders began to heave, and for a moment Emma thought the woman was shaking with laughter. It did sound a bit ridiculous but it wasn't all that funny. Then she realised that her patient was sobbing.

'Oh, Nurse, I'm so worried!'

'There's no need to be, Mrs Mack. You really are making progress now.'

'It's not that, dear, it's my children. I

want to know how they're managing without me. They're not allowed to visit me, so all I can do is sit and fret.'

'You've had to leave them all alone, Mrs Mack?' Emma was horrified.

'Well, not altogether, dear. My Clara, she's fourteen and well able to see to things, but she goes out to work and has to leave our Polly in charge.'

'And how old is she?'

'Eleven. She's had to stay off school to look after the baby.'

'And isn't there anyone who can come, just until you get home again?'

'Not really. My sister lives up in Derby, and there's nobody else. There's old Mrs Sykes in the upstairs flat. I suppose they could go to her in an emergency, but she doesn't really like children. Always calling down the stairs at them to be quiet.'

'I'll have a word with the hospital almoner, if you like,' Emma offered. 'Perhaps she could send someone round to see what's going on there.'

'I don't suppose our Polly would let

them in, if they came round looking all official, like. She'd think it was the rent collector and hide.'

Obviously this was the usual procedure. Emma tried to keep a straight face and almost succeeded. 'I'm sure everything will be all right,' she soothed, taking Mrs Mack's hand in her own. She knew how important it was for the patient not to fret if she was to make a full recovery.

'You couldn't go round and have a look, could you, Nurse?' Mrs Mack's eyes were full of pleading. Emma had seldom seen anyone with such a woebegone expression.

She hesitated. 'Well I suppose I could pop round tomorrow. It will be too late when I get off duty tonight.'

The patient's look of gratitude was a reward in itself.

Emma struggled with her conscience, wondering if she needed to mention this to Sister. Was she doing the right thing in going to check on the youngsters? It seemed like a kind thing to do, but if she found that they were in difficulties, what would she do then? Mrs Mack was sure to ask about them, and it certainly wouldn't help the woman if the news was bad. Well, she would cross that bridge when she came to it.

* * *

Next morning she was off duty between ten o'clock and one, a shift much favoured by the nurses because it meant they could have an early lunch in a cafe, beans on toast or something equally delectable.

She found the tenement building without difficulty, and made her way to the door of the Macks' flat, wishing she could have afforded to buy some little treat for the children. When she arrived she found a man, bent double, trying to peer through the letter box. He straightened up when he heard her.

With a shock she recognised the young doctor from the hospital, the one whom Mrs Mack had described as a real catch. He smiled. 'Don't I know you from somewhere?' he asked.

Emma blushed. 'Yes, Doctor. I'm on women's medical, at St Bee's.'

'Ah, yes, of course. You don't look quite the same without your nurse's veil. I'm James Townsend. Have you come here to check up on Mrs Mack's brood? It appears that we're both on the same errand, but young Polly doesn't seem inclined to let us in. Why don't you call through the letter box? She may be reassured by a woman's voice.'

'Who is it?' A wavering voice came from the other side of the door.

'I'm Nurse Meadows. I've been looking after your mother in the hospital.'

The door was flung open and a young girl stood on the threshold, looking scared. 'Mum's not worse, is she?'

'Your mother is on the mend,' James said.

'How would you know.'

'Because I'm her doctor, that's how.'

'I thought you'd come to tell me she was dead!' Tears began to roll down the child's white cheeks.

James squatted down so that his face was level with hers. 'No, no. Your Mum is a bit worried, that's all, wondering how you were managing. She'll get better a lot faster once she knows you're all right.'

When they had seen that all was well with the baby, and said their goodbyes, James led the way to a battered car. 'Hop in, Nurse!'

Emma hesitated. 'I don't know if I should, Doctor,' she began.

'Don't tell me you mean to walk all the way back to the hospital, Nurse. You'll be exhausted before you even go back on duty, and we can't have that, can we?'

'Well, perhaps if you let me off round the corner,' she murmured. Matron's office overlooked the front entrance, and the woman would have forty fits if she saw one of her nurses alighting from a doctor's car.

James Townsend was a delightful young man and he charmed Emma with his talk of life in the doctors' residence. The drive back to the hospital went all too quickly, and before she knew it he had drawn his car to a halt on Esmonde Street. Rather sadly she watched him as he drove away, leaving her standing on the pavement. She would have liked to see him again, but she knew that was too much to hope for.

3

Storm clouds were brewing that had nothing to do with the war. 'I took a look inside Pierce's satchel, and I didn't like what I found,' Will remarked, his mouth set in a stern line. Rose knew that look of old and she understood it was time to tread carefully.

'Didn't you, dear?'

'I certainly did not! His rough book, which should have been used for taking down notes, or details of homework assignments, is full of silly little sketches of those newfangled flying machines. If this is how he spends his time in class, no wonder he's falling behind!'

Rose bit her lip. She could remember her own school days, when sketches of the latest fashions had to be hastily wiped off her slate before the teacher saw them!

Will saw her guilty look. 'I suppose

you're thinking that you did much the same, and you've turned out all right,' he said, smiling at his pretty wife.

She laughed in return. 'You know me too well. But try not to be too hard on Pierce, dear. He's only a boy.'

'It's for his own good, Rose. It's not too late for him to pull his socks up. As I said, I'll try to find a tutor for him. That should set the boy straight'

Rose's mouth drooped. 'Can we afford that on top of his school fees? Surely you can give him the help he needs. You are a teacher, after all.'

Her husband shook his head. 'And have him argue with me on every issue? No, no, an outsider will be best, someone who won't stand any nonsense. Not another word, Rose. My mind is made up.'

But Rose knew her husband all too well. There was a soft heart behind that stern exterior. 'Whatever you say, dear,' she murmured, doing her best to hide a smile.

When the slam of the back door

heralded the arrival of her only son, Rose made herself scarce. 'Coo-ee, Mum! What time's tea?'

'Never mind that, I want to see you in my study,' Will told him.

'All right, Dad. Actually, there's something I want to ask you about.'

'Come along then,' Will said. 'I think I know what you want to say.' This was more like it. The boy had seen the error of his ways and whom should he turn to for help but his father, the local headmaster?

Unfortunately poor Will was in for a shock.

Busily slicing bread in the kitchen, Rose paused when she heard raised voices. What on earth was going on? Probably Will was laying down the law, while their son was delivering back answers! Although she had made up her mind not to interfere, curiosity overcame her scruples and she tip-toed to the study door where she strained her ears to hear what was going on.

'Don't you understand, boy? You

have a responsibility to all the boys who would have loved to win a place to grammar school, but weren't given the chance. You owe it to them to do well in your chosen profession, whatever that may be.'

'I agree, Dad! It's just that I don't want to be a stuffy old solicitor or accountant. I want to be a pilot. It's the way of the future. That's what it says in the Boy's Own Paper.'

'Stuff and nonsense!'

Unable to bear it any longer, Rose burst into the room. Her husband looked up at her wearily. 'I can't do a thing with the young fool, Rose! You talk to him. I give up!' Picking up his pipe, her husband walked out of the room without a backward glance.

'Pierce Meadows, how could you upset your poor father in this way?'

'But I only asked him if I could take flying lessons, and he completely went off the deep end.'

'Flying lessons! What on earth for?'

It was the wrong thing to say. Pierce

launched into an animated speech about biplanes, whatever they were, and how at this very moment they were being used in the war. The Germans had someone called the Red Baron who seemed to be the leader of something called the Flying Circus. 'Our side have the Royal Flying Corps, of course,' Pierce said proudly.

It all sounded like something one might see in a penny dreadful. Rose couldn't make head or tail of it all. What she did understand was that Pierce often got hold of wild enthusiasms, which all fell by the wayside as soon as something more exciting came along. In his day he had wanted to be a fireman, the operator of a hand-operated lift, and the driver of a brewer's dray. The trick was to let things run their course.

'Are you listening, Mum?'

'Of course, dear. Now, why don't you go and find your father, and make your peace with him, like a good boy.'

'But he's going to find some beastly

tutor, turn me into an awful swot!'

'Oh, I doubt if that will happen,' Rose told him, smiling.

'But the money, Mum! What a waste, when it could buy flying lessons!'

'Oh, do be your age, Pierce!'

'Oh, Mum! A boy at school told me about his uncle. He's been taking lessons. There's an aerodrome at Carleton Heath. I could bike over there.'

Rose's blood ran cold. What, let her only son go up in one of those contraptions? They were nothing more than bits and pieces held together with string, as far as she could tell. Keep calm, she told herself, swallowing hard. 'We're not the sort of people who can afford to do things like that, dear. If you really mean to do this, why don't you get yourself a little job after school and on weekends, and start saving up?'

'And where am I supposed to find the time, if I'm getting this beastly tutor?' Pierce sounded bitter.

'You work hard, and get good qualifications, and when you're out in the working world you'll be able to please yourself what you do with your money — after you pay me for your keep, of course.'

'You don't understand!' Pierce rushed from the room, almost knocking her aside in his haste. She contemplated going after him, but a horrid smell of burning brought her to her senses. 'My shepherd's pie!' she wailed.

Towser followed her hopefully as she made a dash for the kitchen. 'You're in luck, old boy,' she told him. 'Shepherd's pie! Singed, but good enough for dogs. It will have to be scrambled eggs for the rest of us.' The dog licked his lips in anticipation.

An hour later, Will Meadows followed his wife out to the kitchen, where she had put the kettle on to boil. She was glad to see that he appeared calmer now, whereas the meal had been eaten in what could only be described as a fraught silence. Pierce had shovelled his food down as if he were stoking a boiler, and when he stood up he was still gulping and chewing. Without waiting for permission to leave the table he fled from the room and they heard him pounding up the stairs to his bedroom.

'That boy's table manners don't improve,' his father growled, but Rose had wisely refrained from scolding the boy. If Pierce had answered back it might have provoked another outburst from Will that she could do without.

'I think the boy knows where he stands now,' Will said, as the kettle came to a boil. 'He'll soon forget all that rubbish about having flying lessons. Aeroplanes are nothing but a nine days' wonder, Rose. They may have their uses now, while there's a war on, but they'll all go for scrap when things get back to normal.'

'I'm sure you're right, dear,' Rose murmured. 'Now, more tea?'

★ ★ ★

Blissfully unaware of the pandemonium going on at home, young Lucy cycled madly down the road to Priory Farm. Some people thought the land must have belonged to an order of monks originally, until it had been taken from them by King Henry VIII in the sixteenth century. In fact, a local historian had once 'got up on his hind legs' as Farmer Abbot put it, and said as much, at a meeting of the local heritage society. In fact, as Mr Abbot explained later, it was all a bit of a joke, started by his great grandfather in old King William's day.

The old man had made a good marriage with a neighbour's daughter, who brought a hundred acres with her as a dowry. With the two farms joined together as one, it was necessary to come up with a new name, and with an Abbot in charge, Priory Farm seemed eminently suitable!

While none of that meant much to Lucy, she did have an interest in Seth Abbot's son, Adam. For the present this was a deep secret, not to be shared with even her closest friends, but at the age of sixteen she was caught in the throes of first love, and it was wonderful.

The two sets of parents were close friends and all their lives the children had been in and out of each others' houses, much closer than cousins. Adam, much to his mother's sorrow, was an only child. She had married fairly late in life and, having given up all hope of motherhood, she had been overjoyed when Adam put in an appearance. By then it was too late to give him a brother or sister, so when the Meadows children appeared in due course he gravitated towards their home, where he was included in all their activities. In return, they spent many happy hours at the farm, helping with the haymaking and assisting Mrs Abbot to bring up orphaned lambs.

Adam, because he was that much older than the Meadows children, had become their natural leader. Depending on their game of choice he was the pirate chief or the demon king, and when they went through a phase of being Robin Hood and his merry men, Emma played Maid Marian to his Robin. Lucy was the tag-along little sister, only included because her mother insisted that Emma must look after her when they all went out in the fields and woods to play.

Exasperated by the child's incessant demands, Emma and Pierce had, regrettably, tied four-year-old Lucy to a tree on one occasion, telling her that she was a fair maiden who had to wait until someone came to rescue her from the dragon who was lurking nearby. Confident that her hero would come to release her, Lucy sucked her thumb while she complacently watched the others playing some mysterious game. Old Shep the collie, masquerading as the fire-breathing dragon, flopped down beside her to keep her company. Lucy was not in the least frightened, and when at last Adam came to release her, as she had known he would, she gazed up at him with adoring eyes.

Lucy smiled to herself, remembering. Adam was a sturdy young man now, twenty-three years old and committed to the farming life. Perhaps he wasn't tall, dark and handsome, like the heroes in the penny novelettes she revelled in, but he was most attractive nonetheless. His face radiated good health, and he was sun-tanned and wind-blown from being outdoors in all winds and weathers. No doubt about it, he was her ideal man.

'Anybody home?' She put her head around the kitchen door, not quite liking to walk in without an invitation.

'Out here, Lucy,' came a faint call in response.

'Hello, Aunt Lizzie!' Lucy made her way to an outhouse, where Adam's mother was busy candling eggs.

'Hello, dear. You're a bit early, if you've come to help with the milking.'

'I know, but there was nothing to do at home, so here I am.' Lucy watched in fascination as each egg was held up to the light of a candle to make sure it was good enough to send to market.

'If you like you can pack those cracked ones,' Mrs Abbot told her. 'There's plenty of people glad to buy them at half price. Times are hard with so many men away at the war. Housewives trying to make ends meet need all the help they can get.'

Lucy cradled an egg lovingly in her cupped hands. A small downy feather still clung to its ivory-hued shell. What a little miracle an egg is, she thought. Perfect in its own way, like so many things on a farm.

'There, that's done for another week,' Lizzie Abbot exclaimed, straightening her tired back. 'I think I deserve a cup of tea before we start on the milking. And I baked bread this morning, and there's freshly churned butter, and a jar of honey. What do you reckon to that?'

'Lovely!' Lucy said.

Mrs Abbot smiled. She worked hard from dawn until dusk, but she found great satisfaction in the tasks she did, and she was a happy woman.

'How are your parents?' she asked, when they were sitting at the kitchen table with their steaming cups of tea in front of them. 'I haven't seen Rose for a day or two.'

'Dad's none too cheerful, I'm afraid. Almost every day now he seems to find one of his old boys in the casualty lists. It upsets him, I know.'

'Of course it does. Young lads, some of them not much older than you are, Lucy, cut off in their prime. Don't ask me why that Kitchener man talks about them dying a glorious death. Slaughter, that's all it is, and don't you try to tell me otherwise.'

'You must be glad that Adam doesn't have to go.'

'That I am, child, but someone has to stay behind to feed the country. And here we are, working twice as hard, because all the fit young men are leaving us. Left with weak women and old gaffers to carry on, that's us!'

Lucy grinned. Lizzie Abbot could hardly be described as a weak woman. Rose was fond of saying that her friend did the work of three men on the farm, and furthermore she expected everyone else to do the same.

'Your Mum must be worried about young Pierce,' Lizzie said suddenly.

'Pierce? No, why should she be worried about him?'

'Well, he's seventeen, isn't he? Old enough to go and join up, soon.'

'Oh, Mum says the war will be over before he leaves school.' Lucy spoke with confidence. 'He has to get his exams under his belt before he can think of doing anything else.'

'Adam was in the pub last night, and he heard that several of the grammar school boys have chucked in their studies and gone off to take the King's shilling, as they put it. Of course, they all think it's a big adventure. They've seen the new recruits marching through the streets to the tune of a brass band, feeling like heroes with cheering crowds waving flags as they pass by. They've no idea what's ahead of them. They'll get a shock when they get to the front and find out what it's really like.'

Lizzie felt sorry when she saw her young friend's frightened face.

'Sorry, gal, I didn't mean to ramble on like this! Your Pierce would never do anything so silly. Besides, he's not in the top form like those other lads, is he? And he knows that your dad wants him to get into the university.'

'Pierce hasn't said anything to me about wanting to join the army,' Lucy admitted, 'so I expect it's all right.'

'Where on earth are those men of mine?' Lizzie said suddenly, looking at the clock on the wall. 'Adam isn't back from the blacksmith's yet. Old Molly cast a shoe and he had to ride her down slowly. I suppose he had to wait his turn, unless he got talking and lost track of time. But Seth should have been in half an hour ago. He always wants a stay-bit before we start the chores. I can't imagine what's keeping him. Go out and give him a dingle, will you?'

Outside the back door a large metal triangle hung suspended from a tree. Lucy took up the metal rod which lay beside it and beat on it briskly. The sound echoed through the farmyard, but there was no answering cry from Uncle Seth. Puzzled, she repeated her actions, but there was still no response. Lizzie frowned when Lucy returned to the house. "That's odd. You'd think he'd at least have come to the door of the byre to give you a wave. What's he playing at, eh?'

'Could he have gone to the post office? He might be out of baccy.'

Lizzie shook her head. 'Not without letting me know first. And he certainly wouldn't want to smoke in the byre, not with all that straw around! Your legs are younger than mine. Run down and see what's keeping him, will you?'

Lucy sped across the farmyard, noticing that the cows were patiently making their way across the fields in a long line, heading for the five-barred gate which would admit them into the yard, ready for the milking shed.

With one hand on the latch of the barn door she called out tentatively, 'Uncle Seth! Are you there? Aunt Lizzie wants to know if you want your tea.'

No reply. She opened the door and peered into the gloom. Up at the far end there was a ladder leading to the hay loft above, and at the bottom of this, Seth Abbott was lying on the floor in a crumpled heap.

For a long moment Lucy swayed, fighting of a feeling of faintness. Was he dead? She wanted to call to Aunt Lizzie, but she didn't know if her legs would carry her that far, so rubbery did they feel. With her heart in her mouth she edged forward.

'Uncle Seth! Are you all right?' Of all the silly questions, that had to take the prize, she told herself, but she didn't know what else to do.

He groaned, and struggled to raise his head to look at her. 'One of the rungs gave way underneath me, and I came a cropper,' he whispered. 'I've been lying here I don't know how long, but nobody came. Somehow I didn't have the strength to shout. I can't move much, and I think I've broken my back. Can you run and fetch the doctor, child?'

Gulping, Lucy straightened up and ran for the open door.

4

Jenny's eyes opened wide as she took in what her room mate had just told her. 'You mean he actually spoke to you? Dr James Townsend spoke to you!'

'He could hardly avoid it,' Emma said, laughing. 'We were both standing on the doorstep, trying to convince Mrs Mack's little girl that we were not rent collectors, and he told me that I'd better try to get through to her. He thought she might trust me, as I'm female.'

'Aren't there any female rent collectors, then?'

'Fool! He was quite right, though. She did co-operate when I explained that I'm nursing her mummy. Honestly, it was enough to break a person's heart. There she was, only eleven years old, all on her own, having to stay home from school to look after a baby. No wonder

Mrs Mack is worried.'

'And do they have to stay alone at night, then? That's awful!'

'There's a fourteen year old, apparently, who goes out to work by day, and I expect she sleeps in the flat with the younger ones. I don't know where the other children were when we called. At school, I suppose. There are six altogether, though the place looked tidy enough, for a place without any adult supervision.'

'Oh, well, they seem to be managing, then. A lot of people are worse off. But what about Dr Townsend?'

'What about him?'

'Do you know, Emma Meadows, you can be really annoying at times!'

Emma took pity on her friend. 'Well, he drove me back to the hospital.'

Jenny squealed. 'In his car?'

'No, silly, in his pumpkin!'

'But what if Matron had seen you? She'd have had you on the carpet before you could say Cinderella!'

'I asked him to drop me on the

corner. Matron will never hear about it.'

'That's what you think! You can bet your boots that you were seen by somebody! And everyone will want to know who the girl was with the dishy Dr Townsend. So, is he as nice as he looks? Are you going to see him again? Has he asked you out?'

'No, no, and no again,' Emma said, laughing indulgently at her friend. 'I'm sorry to have to disappoint you, but there really is nothing to report.'

'Shame!'

Emma had to agree. Still, Mrs Mack's response when she heard that all was well at home more than made up for any disappointment.

'Oh, Nurse! I don't know how to thank you! And everything was all right, was it? How is our Polly managing? And the baby — still teething, is he? Are they all finding enough to eat? And has that dratted rent man been round?'

Doing her best to deal with the volley of questions, Emma failed to notice Dr

Townsend striding down the long ward, with Sister fluttering in his wake.

'Why, look who's here, Nurse!' Mrs Mack's face lit up when she saw the handsome young doctor. Emma's heart sank. Any minute now, she'd find herself in deep trouble. The woman had only to let drop that the pair of them had met outside the hospital and the sky would fall.

But the doctor forestalled any injudicious remark Mrs Mack might make. 'Thank you, Sister. I just want a quick word with my patient. I shan't be staying long.'

Thus dismissed, Sister glared at Emma. 'Where have those two probationers got to? That sluice is a disgrace! Go and roust them out at once. And if I find they've been smoking, I shall send the pair of them straight to Matron!'

'Yes, Sister! Right away, Sister!' Emma scurried off, keen to get away. But later, when she was hastening down the ward, she almost collided with Dr Townsend, who was marching towards

45

the door. Smothering a gasp she stepped back, just in time to avoid crashing into him. He winked at her, causing her heart to flutter.

How romantic was that! She had just run into the man of her dreams — literally — and there she was, carrying a smelly bedpan! Just what every girl needs, she thought ruefully. Of course, being a doctor, he wasn't likely to be put off by a little thing like that, but it didn't mean that he thought of her as anything other than Mrs Mack's little nurse. She could imagine the sort of woman he would like to have on his arm when he went to some posh event. Someone with impeccable make-up and not a hair out of place, wearing clothes the likes of which Emma could never afford.

She caught sight of Mrs Mack, signalling wildly. She pointed to the bedpan, indicating that she must deal with that first. Mrs Mack gave her a thumbs-up sign. Emma knew what this was all about, and she shrank from what she guessed was coming; a discussion of the merits of Dr James Townsend! Still, she couldn't ignore the woman, or Sister would want to know the reason why!

'Fancy that!' Mrs Mack said when Emma finally reached her side.

'What's that, Mrs Mack?'

'Why, love, you and the doctor turning up on my doorstep at the same time. That was fate, that was!'

'Are you sure you didn't have something to do with that, Mrs Mack?'

The woman was the picture of wide-eyed innocence. 'Would I do such a thing? I might have mentioned to him how worried I was, about my kiddies being left all alone, and what mother worth her salt wouldn't be? But trying to fix it so you two would be there at the same time, how could I have done that, eh? You never said what time you'd be going, did you?'

'I suppose not.' Emma had to admit that, worried as the woman was, it was only natural that she'd mention her concerns to as many people as possible, in the hope that someone would do something about the situation.

'Anyway,' Mrs Mack went on, 'where's the harm, love? Now you two know each other, something good may come of it, eh?'

'What do you mean by that?' Emma pretended to smooth the bed sheets. Sister had eyes in the back of her head, and to be caught standing gossiping was a sin of the worst order.

'Why, here's the pair of you, both unattached, working in the same place. Seems to me someone needs to bring you two together.'

'How do you know he's unattached, then?'

Mrs Mack chuckled. 'Because I asked him, that's why! How else is a person to know how the land lies, unless she asks? Now then, next time you see him, you go up to him and say that I'm that worried about the kiddies, I can't eat nor sleep. You tell him the pair of you better get back to the flat and make sure everything's still all right.'

'Oh, I couldn't possibly do that!'

'Why ever not? You like him, don't you? Where's the harm? Faint heart never won fair gentleman.'

'I've explained before, Mrs Mack. He's a qualified doctor, I'm a trainee nurse, and never the twain shall meet!'

'A lot of rot, that is! Why else would a nice girl like you come to a place like this, where they work you like a cart horse? They make you do things that no girl in service would lower herself to do, unless she was a poor little skivvy with no choice.'

'What we do here is all part of ministering to the sick,' Emma said, hoping she wasn't sounding too pious. 'And I became a nurse because I want to help people.'

'That's all well and good, Nurse Meadows, but what's the point of it all? Once you're married they won't let you work at it any more. Isn't that what you told me?'

'That's true. Nobody could work twelve hours a day here and have time left to look after a husband and children.'

'That's what I thought. So you want to marry well, don't you, and I've found just the man for you, Nurse.'

'Go on with you, Mrs Mack!' Laughing, Emma went away to tackle the next task on her list. She had no intention of chasing after James Townsend, or any other doctor, for that matter. She was attracted to the man, yes, who wouldn't be? But she had other fish to fry. She wanted to complete her training and receive her diploma and the coveted blue and silver badge that would proclaim her a graduate of St Botolph's.

After that, she wasn't sure. She might stay on here for a time, if she were to be offered a position as Staff Nurse. Or, in time, she might return to Hartscombe, if the post of District Nurse became available. She would enjoy visiting patients in their homes. She might even do midwifery training; helping to bring new babies into the world would be most satisfying.

Many of her set had vowed to serve in France when they were old enough. You had to be twenty-three to sign on. Emma knew she was no heroine and she didn't think she could face that. Besides, somebody had to nurse on the home front, didn't they? People still got sick, and broke bones, and needed operations.

But despite all her plans for the future, Emma knew, deep inside that in the unlikely event that James asked her out, she would go. Oh, yes, she certainly would!

5

Having come out on the step, Lizzie Abbot waited impatiently for Lucy to reappear. What on earth were the two of them playing at? Seth had a pocket watch, so why hadn't he come in for his cup of tea? He must know that it was almost time to start the milking!

Ah, here they were at last! She smiled as she saw Lucy rushing out of the barn. But the girl signalled to her, arms waving like a windmill, before dashing for her bicycle and charging off. And there was still no sign of Seth!

'Please, God, not a heart attack!' she whispered, hurling herself down the steps to the path below. She flew over to the barn and hurtled through the main door, which Lucy had left open. 'Seth! Seth! Are you all right?'

'Over here, love.' She hardly recognized her husband's voice, so different from his usual deep tones.

'Oh, Seth, what have you done to yourself?' Lizzie sank down beside him, trying to hold back the tears,

'Fell down that dratted ladder, didn't I? Can't seem to move my legs. I've sent young Lucy to fetch the doctor to me. Then we'll see what's what.'

'It's times like this I wish we had one of those telephones,' Lizzie murmured, cradling her husband's head in her lap.

'Newfangled contraptions aren't for the likes of us.'

'There's no denying they could come in handy at a time like this.'

'It doesn't matter. The post office isn't that far off, and I suppose that's where Lucy's heading.'

'But they'll be shut at this time of day,' Lizzie wailed.

'She can go round to the side door and Mrs Mapstone will let her in. Don't you fret, my love. It will all come out in the wash.'

Lizzie could hardly bear it. Her poor husband might be badly injured, yet he still found the strength to reassure her, when it should have been the other way round. In her mind she said a fervent prayer that he'd be all right.

Lucy, meanwhile, was pedalling down the lane as hard as she could go. It was with a sigh of relief that she saw Adam, leading the cart horse.

'Where are you off to in such a hurry, young 'un?' he asked, grinning at her as she put down one foot to stop the bicycle.

'Uncle Seth's had an accident!' she panted. 'Fell off a ladder and now he can't move. I'm going to phone for Doctor Pierce.'

Adam took charge at once. 'Better let me, Lucy. Can you lead old Molly home? Give us your bike, then!'

He pushed away on her antiquated machine, swinging his leg over the saddle as he went. At any other time she'd have been amused at the sight of long-legged Adam cycling along with his knees not far from his chin, but things were too serious for laughter.

Adam was everything she admired in a man, and his ability to sum up a situation and act on it immediately was all part of that. She turned to the horse.

'Come up, girl! Let's get you home.' The horse, knowing that supper awaited her, broke into a trot, and Lucy was forced to do likewise. They burst into the farmyard, just as Lizzie emerged from the barn, anxious to see what was happening.

'I met Adam. He's gone for Doctor Lynch,' Lucy gasped out, before Lizzie had the chance to say anything.

'Thank goodness! Let's hope it won't be long now, then. Can you turn Molly into the paddock? Then you'd better nip off home, gal, or your parents will be wondering what's happened to you.'

'Oh, but I wanted to stay and . . . '

'Not now, child. Run along, there's a good girl.'

Feeling rather put out, Lucy did as she was asked. The cattle, still making their way home, watched her with curious eyes as she let the horse out, carefully closing the gate behind her. She did so want to stay and see what happened next, instead of being treated like a child. If it hadn't been for her the Abbots would have had to wait until Adam arrived and, although he had almost reached home they weren't to know that. Now she'd have to walk all the way home because Adam had her only means of transportation. Feeling disgruntled, she set off down the dusty lane.

'I wasn't expecting you home yet,' was her mother's greeting when she turned in at the gate, feeling dirty and thirsty. 'And where's your bicycle? I hope something hasn't happened to it, Lucy, they cost a lot of money.'

'Adam borrowed it. He had to go for Doctor Lynch.'

'Oh, dear. Nothing's wrong at the farm, I hope.'

'It's Uncle Seth. He fell off a ladder and his back is broken.'

'Come now, dear. Aren't you exaggerating just a bit?' Rose was used to

Lucy's dramatics and had learned not to jump to drastic conclusions.

'That's what Uncle Seth told me. It was me who found him, see?'

'Then we'll just have to hope he's wrong. Well, now that you're here you can peel a few potatoes for me. I must pop in and find your father. He'll want to know what's been happening.'

'All right, Mum.' But Lucy lingered at the gate, hoping to catch a glimpse of Adam returning. As it was she saw Dr Lynch's car speeding by, which gave her some comfort, knowing that help was on its way to poor Seth.

It wasn't until early the following morning that news came. The clip-clop sounds of an approaching horse drew Lucy outside. It was Molly, harnessed to the farm cart, heading in the direction of the schoolhouse.

'Mum! Dad! It's Adam, and I think he's coming here.' She was soon joined by her parents, who waited for Adam to draw up at their gate.

'Hello, all! I've brought your bike

back, Lucy. I'm afraid it got a puncture when I was charging over the cobbles, taking a short cut to Doc's place, but I've mended it now and it should be all right.'

'How is poor Seth?' Rose said. 'He's up and doing now, I hope?'

Adam's mouth drooped. 'I'm afraid not. Didn't you hear the ambulance going by last night?'

'I'm not sure that we did,' William Meadows put in. 'We're so used to hearing horse drawn vehicles passing by, we don't pay much attention. Unless we happened to be looking out at the time, we'd have missed it completely. So Seth has been taken to hospital? What did Dr Lynch say?'

'Apparently Dad has hurt his spine. They don't think that anything is broken; they're hoping that he may just be badly bruised. But at the moment he can't feel his legs, so it looks like it's going to be a long job.'

'That's going to leave you short handed on the farm, isn't it.'

'I'm afraid it is, particularly since Peter has gone to join up. And as far as finding another ag lab to take his place goes, we might as well whistle into the wind. All the able-bodied men from hereabouts have gone to the war.'

'But that just leaves you and your mother to run the place,' Rose exclaimed. 'Will, dear, what about the older boys at the school? Couldn't one or two of them give Adam a hand?'

But Will shook his head. 'They all have enough to do on their parents' farms, Rose. What with that and trying to keep pace with their studies, I don't know where they'd find the time.'

'I'll go,' Lucy announced. 'It can be my war work. I already give you a hand now and then. I can easily come over every day. I know the animals.'

'You can't possibly,' Rose began, but her husband nodded his approval.

'I'm sure you can find Lucy some light work, can't you, my boy? If all else fails she can always be assigned some housekeeping tasks which will free your mother for outside work.'

Working as a glorified parlourmaid was not exactly what Lucy had in mind, but anything that would keep her in close proximity to Adam was all right with her. She nodded enthusiastically.

'Well, if you're sure,' Adam said, looking relieved. 'I'll have a word with Mum and see what she thinks, but I'm sure she'll be delighted to have the extra help. Pop in later in the day, and we'll see what she has to say.'

'Are you sure you won't be taking on too much?' Rose asked, when Adam had gone on his way. 'You know you've always been rather delicate.'

'Oh, Mum! Don't fuss! It doesn't take much strength to gather up the eggs, or to bring the cows home from the pasture. I'm sure that Aunt Lizzie won't have me heaving bales of hay around, or cutting down trees.'

'Then we'll just have to see how things work out, won't we.'

★　★　★

Will Meadows strode into the house in a flaming temper. His wife could tell that by the way he slammed the back door.

Now what? she wondered. The day had started out so peacefully. While he had gone down to the newsagent's to pick up his Saturday paper, Rose had made herself a second cup of tea and had sat down to enjoy it while everything was quiet. Their little maid, Cherry Neale, didn't come in at the weekend, and Rose usually forgot about housework and put in a few hours in the garden. The large vegetable plot was Will's province, but she had her roses and the herb garden, which kept her happy.

The news from the war wasn't good. All the more reason to count her blessings on the home front, she thought. All her children were safe in Gloucestershire; Emma at the hospital, Pierce at home and Lucy helping out down the road at the farm.

But now, judging by the way her

husband was banging around in the back lobby, something had come about to disturb that peace.

'Would you like a cup of tea, dear?' she asked, as he burst into the kitchen. 'I've just made a fresh pot.'

Red-faced, he ignored her. 'That boy! He'll be the death of me!'

'You mean Pierce? He certainly will be the death of you if you don't calm down. We don't want you falling with apoplexy.'

'Pierce! What other boy do we have, eh? You tell me that.'

'What has he done now, then?'

'You may well ask! I ran into old Butler at the shop, and what do you think he told me?'

'That's the man you hired to tutor Pierce?' Rose asked her husband.

'Well, I thought I did!'

'And is Pierce still slacking off?'

'Slacking off! It's worse than that, old girl; much worse!'

Will could feel his blood pressure mounting. He sat down and put his face in his hands, willing himself to calm down. Where had they gone wrong? How had they failed their son? In his mind he replayed the scene at the newsagent's shop. He had been surprised to see Tom Butler standing at the counter, waiting to be served.

'Hello, Butler! Where's Pierce? Shouldn't you be giving him a maths revision? Or have you just popped out for a moment and left him working?'

The man had looked puzzled. 'Pierce? I haven't seen him, Meadows. I've been expecting him every Saturday since we fixed up the arrangement, and I thought you must have changed your mind. You might have let me know, old man. I must say I'm a bit disappointed, for I was rather counting on the fees we agreed on.'

'But I gave the boy the money to pay you in advance! You mean he's never given it to you?'

'Well, no. As I said, I haven't seen him at all.'

Muttering apologies, Will managed to

get out of the shop without venting his fury in front of his former colleague who, of course, was the innocent bystander in all this. But when he caught up with his errant son, he'd have more than a thing or two to say to the boy.

Now he looked up at his wife, while a tear escaped from the corner of his eye. 'That boy, Rose, has lied and cheated. And he's a thief as well.' Stumbling over his words he told her what he'd heard from Tom Butler.

'Our Pierce? Surely not, dear. There has to be a mistake somewhere.'

'Oh, there's been a mistake, all right, and it's Pierce who has made it. Where is the boy now?'

Rose bit her lip. 'As you know, he went out first thing this morning. I naturally assumed that he was on his way to his lesson. He had his satchel with him, and it seemed to be full of books.'

'More lies and cover ups! I'm going for a walk, Rose, to try to calm down, but if that young whippersnapper comes home while I'm out, he's to go straight to his room and wait for me there. Do I make myself clear?'

★ ★ ★

Later, Rose was to ponder that there might be something in the old superstition that trouble always comes in threes, for things became worse as the day wore on. She was surprised when Cherry burst into the kitchen, her eyelids swollen red with weeping.

'What on earth are you doing here on a Saturday, child? Is there something wrong at home? I do hope it's not your mother, is it?'

'Oh, Madam! There's been one of them marconigrams!'

Light dawned. 'Not your Peter!'

'Yes, Madam. Missing in action, it says. Mum can't understand it. How can he be missing? We only had a letter from him yesterday. It must be a mistake, Mum says, so she sent me up here to ask Sir what he thinks.'

'Mr Meadows has gone out for a walk, Cherry. You'd better sit down and have a cup of tea while you wait.'

Poor young Peter, Rose thought. She had known the Neale family since the children were born. They had gone through the local school under Will's supervision, and he had seen them take their places out in the working world. Peter had worked for the Abbots until recently, when he had gone to join up. Now, barely older than Pierce, it seemed he was gone.

'Mum thinks missing is better than dead, Madam, cos it means he could turn up at any moment. Do you think that's true?'

'Anything is possible, dear.'

'Only it's not knowing that's the worst,' Cherry went on. 'And I've got two more brothers over there, and if anything happens to them she'll go mad, I know she will.'

There ought to be a law against it, Rose thought. Making more than one member of a family go off to war is positively inhumane. But she couldn't say that to poor Cherry. Instead, she patted her on the back, murmuring meaningless words of consolation.

Will did no better when he came home and heard Cherry's story, for what was there to say? He advised her to go and see the vicar, who would call on Mrs Neale as he did with all the bereaved mothers. Perhaps it would be some comfort to the poor soul. The girl had no sooner left when they heard someone rapping on the front door.

'Who can that be?' Will wondered, getting up from his chair. 'Has Cherry left something behind?'

'She wouldn't come to the front door, dear. She knows we always come in at the back. It must be a stranger.'

The visitor was a uniformed policeman who had arrived by bicycle. 'Are you Mr William Meadows?'

'Yes, yes, that's right.'

The policeman looked awkward. 'I'm sorry to tell you I'm the bearer of bad news. Your son has been killed, sir.'

'Oh, you've come to the wrong house. My son isn't involved in the war. He's just a schoolboy.'

'This isn't about the war, sir. May I come in?'

Puzzled, and now a little frightened, Will stood aside to let the man in.

'Who is it, Will? Is anything the matter?' Rose came into the hall and frowned when she saw the policeman.

'Sir, madam, can we go somewhere you can sit down? This will come as a shock, I'm afraid.'

Will led the way into the kitchen. He remained standing, although he gently pushed his wife down on to a chair. 'You were saying, Constable?'

'I'm sorry, Sir, but there's been an accident over at Carleton Heath, at the aerodrome. Your son was flying one of their biplanes, when it crashed.'

Rose actually laughed. 'Then someone is properly mixed up! Our boy is not a pilot. Oh, he's mad about those planes, all right, and I suppose it's possible that he's gone to the airfield to watch them coming and going, but that's all there is to it.'

'I'm afraid not, Madam. A call came in to the station, telling us of the unfortunate occurrence, and asking us to inform the next of kin, which is you, Sir. The . . . er . . . your son's body has been taken to the . . . um . . . morgue at St Botolph's, if you know where that is.'

'Yes, we do know where that is. Our daughter is a nurse there.'

When the constable had been shown to the door, obviously relieved at having completed his errand, Will returned to the kitchen, to find his wife on the verge of hysteria. He took her into his arms.

'What are we to do, Will? It has to be a mistake, but if it is, then why doesn't Pierce come home? We must go to the hospital at once, but Gloucester is so far away. How do we get there? The bus only goes twice a week, and the next one isn't until Wednesday!'

'I shall go to the post office and telephone the hospital from there. Once we know more we can make plans. I'll pick up a train timetable at the same time.' Although if the poor boy is in the morgue, there will be no need for us both to go, Will told himself. If it's only a case of identification one of us will be enough. I wouldn't wish to put poor Rose through that.

Left alone in the house, his wife was left with a much better idea of how poor Mrs Neale was feeling, following the news of her son's disappearance. And to think that she had started this day, selfishly feeling glad that her own children were safe here in England. All that was changed now.

★   ★   ★

Emma was in the men's medical ward, standing beside Seth Abbot's bed. Because she was meant to be on duty during visiting hours, the ward sister had allowed her to come to see him during her time off.

'Just for a few minutes, mind, Nurse,

seeing as you're a friend of the family. You shouldn't be here, really, but perhaps you can cheer him up a bit. I understand that his wife and son can't leave the farm to come all the way here, so he's feeling a bit low.'

'Yes, Sister. How is he doing, anyway?'

'There's been some improvement, I'm happy to say. Mr Preston was afraid that there might have been damage to the spinal cord, but the patient is able to move his toes now, and that's an encouraging sign. Perhaps it's just a case of bad bruising after all. Mr Abbot tells me that it was your young sister who found him after he had his accident.'

'Yes. She's helping out on the farm while they're short handed.'

'Good for her. Well, away you go, and you can tidy up his bed while you're at it. It looks like someone's been doing the highland fling on it.'

'Good to see you, love!' Seth said, beaming. 'Any news from home?'

71

'Not for a couple of days now, Uncle Seth. I know that Lucy is delighted to be able to help Aunt Lizzie where she can.'

'She's a good girl, bless her. And I know they can't find any ag labs, not for love nor money. I can't wait till I get out of here.'

'I'm afraid you'll have to be patient for a while longer, Uncle Seth.'

'But how can I, lying here flat on my back, when everything's been left to Lizzie and Adam and a slip of a girl?'

Whatever retort Emma had meant to make was swallowed up by the arrival of an untidy little probationer who addressed her breathlessly.

'Please, are you Nurse Meadows?'

'Yes, I'm Nurse Meadows. Have you been sent to find me? Am I needed back on the ward?' Although Emma was off duty there was always the possibility that she might be called back if some emergency arose, such as a train wreck or an explosion at a munitions factory. In such cases it was all hands to the pump, dealing with the overflow from Casualty.

'Please, nurse, you're to go to Matron's office right away.'

'Uh, oh!' Seth said, grinning. 'What have you done, gal? Broken a thermometer, have you?'

But as she marched down the ward, searching her conscience, she couldn't think of any great sin she might have committed. She hadn't come back to the nurses' home after curfew and she certainly hadn't made any grave error while working on the ward. There was only one possibility, and that was that some busybody had seen her getting out of James Townsend's car, and had reported her to Matron. And that didn't have to be one of her fellow nurses. There were always members of the public willing to pass on tittle tattle, although how such a person could have pegged her as a nurse, since she was in mufti at the time, was anybody's guess.

When she knocked on Matron's door and was bidden to enter, she stepped inside and came face to face with Dr James Townsend. He was the last person she'd expected to see, and it seemed as if her worst fears were about to come true.

'Do sit down, Nurse,' Matron said, indicating a chair. Emma perched on the edge, wondering what was coming next. Surely if she was 'on the carpet' she'd be expected to meet her fate standing up?

'I'm afraid we have bad news, Nurse. Doctor Townsend will explain.'

'Your father has been on the telephone, Nurse,' James began. 'I'm afraid it's your brother. He's had an accident, and was feared dead. However, when he was brought here and examined by Dr Caswell, it transpired that he was merely unconscious. He also has a fractured femur and miscellaneous cuts and bruises.'

'Will he be all right?'

'I'm afraid I can't venture a prognosis until he regains consciousness, but of course you understand that, Nurse.'

'Can I see him?'

'Yes. With Matron's permission, I'll take you to him now.'

'How did you know that Pierce is my brother?' Emma asked, as they walked down the long corridor to the small side ward where Pierce was being monitored.

'Unfortunately your parents were informed by the constabulary that the boy was dead, and brought here to the morgue. Very sensibly your father telephoned here for confirmation, before rushing to Gloucester to view the body. While he was at it he happened to mention that you are working here.'

'Poor Dad. I suppose he thought it might give him access to inside information of some sort. But what kind of accident was it, Doctor Townsend? Was he run over by a motor car or something?'

'From the little information I have, I gather that he was piloting some sort of aircraft, which crashed.'

'That's wrong, for a start!' Emma

cried. 'He's not in the Royal Flying Corps; he's only a schoolboy.'

'I expect somebody took him up for a ride.'

'But they go up quite high, don't they? Nobody could fall out of the sky and not be killed. Oh, there's a mixup somewhere.'

'We shan't know until he regains consciousness.'

'If he regains consciousness!'

They had arrived at the door of the little ward now and, seeing the doctor, a probationer jumped up from the chair where she had been sitting to monitor the boy's vital signs.

'Has he come round yet, Nurse?'

'He hasn't stirred since they brought him in, Doctor.'

Emma looked down at the familiar face of her brother, on which several cuts stood out in scarlet relief against his white cheeks.

'Oh, Pierce,' she murmured. It was one thing to remain dispassionate about the patients and their injuries because you were not emotionally involved with them. It was quite another when it was a member of your own family in extremis.

'There's nothing more you can do here, Nurse, so I'm taking you down to the dining hall for a well-sugared cup of tea,' James told her.

'Oh, but you can't,' she stammered.

'I certainly can. Doctor's orders,' Dr Townsend insisted firmly but kindly.

'You're very kind, but people will talk.'

'Then what about that little cafe around the corner? We're both off duty, both in mufti. Take pity on me, Nurse Meadows — I'd love to get out of this place for half an hour. What's your first name, by the way? I suppose you must have one.'

'Emma.'

'Then come along, Emma.'

In a daze, she followed him outside, her mind buzzing with unanswered questions, not the least of which was what had really happened to Pierce.

As they sipped their tea, James put himself out to be charming to her, and she was glad to be distracted. He told her about his home in St Albans, where his father was a GP and his mother busy bringing up his five sisters. In turn she told him about her own family, and he nodded pleasantly.

'I'll look forward to meeting your parents when they arrive, Nurse. I'm sure our mothers would have a lot in common, what with all that knitting and bandage rolling they do for the war effort.'

Later that day Emma, once more in uniform, reported back on duty. She was surprised when Sister Martin bustled up to her, wearing a toothy smile.

'What are you doing here, Nurse? Didn't you get my message?'

'No, Sister. What message was that?'

'Why, that you mustn't come back on duty today. We've heard all about your brother and Matron tells me that your parents are on their way here. She thought you'd like to spend some time with them and I'm sure they'd be glad to see you.'

'That's very kind of Matron, Sister, but I'd prefer to keep busy, at least until they get here.'

'No, Nurse. I must insist. You're bound to be distressed, and in that state you could make mistakes, and that I won't have. Off you go now. Put your feet up and have a nice read.'

It was just as well that she'd been excused duty, Emma thought, as she plodded her way over to the nurses' home, for she'd never be able to concentrate on anything until she knew if Pierce was going to be all right.

She was greeted by Home Sister, who had apparently been warned of her coming. 'Into bed with you, my girl, and I'll fetch you some hot milk. What you need is a nice nap while you're waiting for your parents to arrive.'

★　★　★

'The first thing is, he's not dead,' Will said.

'Are you sure?' Rose raised a woeful face to her husband. She had been crying since he'd gone off to telephone, and she knew she must present a pretty picture of woe! Still, what did that matter, if her boy was alive?

'I don't know about you, but I need a stiff drink,' Will told her. 'We'll have a little tot and then we'll sit down and try to make sense of this whole sorry business.' He went to fetch the bottle of brandy they kept for medicinal emergencies. And what was this if not an emergency of the worst kind?

'But this aeroplane business,' Rose said, when she'd taken a sip or two of her brandy, pretending not to notice that Will had knocked his back in one long swig. 'Was he really up in the air all by himself, or was somebody else driving the thing?'

'I got on to the manager, or the commodore or whatever the chap calls himself, at Carleton Heath. They give

80

flying lessons, and they also take people up on what they call joy rides. It seems that Pierce turned up there one day and went for a spin. Since then he's been returning every Saturday to take lessons, and this week it was his first solo flight.'

'Oh, Will!' Rose's hand went to her mouth. 'But surely flying lessons are very expensive? Where on earth would he find the money?'

'Where do you think? It must have been the cash I gave him to pay Tom Butler. The boy is a thief, Rose. A liar and a thief!'

'I can't bear it, Will, I just can't bear it.'

'Then how do you think I feel? We've done our best to keep him on the straight and narrow, so how has it come to this? And see where all this has got him. Lying on a morgue slab, that's where.'

'But what actually happened, did they say?'

'Apparently he was about to take off,

trundling down the runway, when something went wrong. Either the machine malfunctioned in some way, or the boy became muddled, who knows? In any case the aircraft never became airborne, and that's what saved his life. It just lifted a few feet off the ground and then it sort of flipped over, or so I understand. When they got to the boy they really thought he was dead. He wasn't moving, and they didn't think he was breathing. Luckily they sent for medical help right away and he was taken to St Botolph's, in a motor ambulance. I've been on to them there and the doctors believe he'll survive, although what sort of state he'll be in when he wakes up they weren't prepared to say.'

'We must go to him at once, Will. I must be there when he comes round.'

'There's a train at nine in the morning. We'll take that.'

'Did they let you speak to Emma?'

'I didn't ask. No doubt she has her work to do. Do you want to know what

I think about all this, Rose?' Without waiting for an answer he went on, 'I think that the wretched boy was planning to sneak off to join this Flying Corps without saying a word to us. He'd have lied about his age to get in, and presented himself as a qualified pilot to get them to take him on.'

'He'd never have gone away without telling me,' Rose said.

'Oh, no? Did he tell you he'd stolen Butler's tutoring fees to pay for this training? No, of course he didn't! I tell you, Rose, when he wakes up he's going to get the telling off of his life, and he needn't think otherwise.'

'Quite right, dear,' Rose told him, but inwardly she was rejoicing. With the injuries Pierce had received in this accident, he would never be fit for military service now. If only he could recover and be able to live a normal life, he would be safe from harm, under his mother's wing. As far as she was concerned, the money the boy had misappropriated was money well spent.

* * *

When they arrived at the hospital they were met by a kindly ward sister, who impressed them as a most capable woman. She shared the news that Pierce had come round for a few minutes and had been asking for his mother. 'And when he's fully conscious the doctors will be dealing with his fractured femur, which will have to go into traction.'

'What does that mean exactly?' Will asked.

'It means he'll have to lie on his back with the injured leg elevated by pulleys. That part of his recovery will take three to four months. After that he'll have to learn to walk again, so I'm afraid he won't be coming home for a while yet,' she explained.

'You have our next door neighbour here, I believe,' Rose said. 'Uncle Seth, as Pierce calls him. Perhaps their beds could be put side by side? They'd be company for each other.'

Sister nodded pleasantly, but Will noticed that she made no promises. This was her domain and she ruled the roost. Emma had told them how strictly the nursing sisters ran their wards. Discipline here was every bit as strict as it was in the army, and Matron was the general in charge.

Some hours later, when they were settled in and had returned for visiting hours, he was impressed when a young nurse came in to greet them, her apron crackling with starch, and he realised that it was his own daughter underneath the flowing veil.

'Mum, Dad, you're here!'

'Oh, Emma, I'm so glad to see you!' Rose burst into tears.

'The worst is over now, Mum. Are they finding you somewhere to stay?'

'The almoner sent us to a house just over the road,' Will confirmed. 'A woman there takes in people from out of town who have someone in the hospital. Our room is rather spartan but it will do us for now. A hotel would have been far too expensive on top of our fares and meals.'

'That's all right then. Have you been in to see Pierce?'

'They let us have a quick peek at him when we first arrived,' Rose said. 'We're going to sit with him now. How long before he comes round?'

'Any minute now, I should think,' Emma assured her. 'And I suppose you'll give him a good talking to when he does, Dad?'

'The young fool deserves more than a scolding,' Will said grimly, but Emma knew that he was only too thankful to find his son alive, especially when they'd been told at first that her brother had died in the crash.

'That nice young man of yours has been to see us,' Rose said now. 'Why didn't you tell us you were walking out with someone?'

'Young man? Walking out? I don't know what you're talking about.' Emma knew that she was blushing.

'Of course you do, dear. And he's

invited us all out to lunch tomorrow at a restaurant down the road.'

'But I . . . '

'Don't be silly, dear. He knows you're free because he's spoken to the sister on your ward.'

'Is this Doctor Townsend you're talking about?'

'Of course it is, dear. How many young men do you have on your string?'

Emma didn't know what to say. It was no good trying to explain things to Mum. She was a product of Hartscombe, where everything was so simple. If a young man fancied a girl he would ask her out, and in time meet her parents. It was nothing like the rigid etiquette of hospital life.

Mum, of course, had jumped to conclusions. Just because James was kind enough to befriend them in their hour of need it didn't mean that he was seriously interested in their daughter. Nor would he have suggested that he was Emma's 'young man'. On the other hand, he could hardly make a habit of taking out all the relations of St Bee's patients, could he?

★　★　★

Next day at the restaurant, James urged the Meadows to order anything they fancied. Will insisted on paying part of the bill; he rightly surmised that this young man did not have a great deal of money to burn. He had not been qualified for long enough to be making the salary that more senior doctors enjoyed. This became apparent when Will questioned him about his work.

'I qualified at St Thomas's Hospital in London, Mr Meadows. I've come to St Bee's to take further surgical training before I go to France. While I'm waiting to start I'm helping out here and there in the hospital because they're short handed with so many doctors having already gone overseas.'

Emma felt an unpleasant lurch in the pit of her stomach. So he was only here for a short time, and then the war would claim him. Life was so unfair! She poked gloomily at her fish, her appetite suddenly gone, while James and her father discussed the progress of the war. Turning to her mother, she recognized a certain look in that lady's eye.

'Beatrice Halliwell is getting married next week,' Rose remarked, this being a girl with whom Emma had gone to school. 'Her mother wanted her to wait until the war is over but she is determined to marry before her husband leaves for France. What do you think about it, Emma?'

'I think it's most unwise,' Emma retorted, hoping to forestall any embarrassing comments her mother might make in front of James Townsend.

6

Pierce came back to life, in pain and more than a little confused. 'Mum! Is that you? What happened? Am I in a hospital?'

'Yes, darling, you've had an accident, but you're going to be all right.'

'What sort of accident? Did I come off my bike?'

'I'm not surprised he can't remember anything,' Will grunted. 'Then he'd have to face the music.'

But Sister explained that it was not unusual for patients with a bump on the head to suffer partial amnesia. 'And since the aeroplane crash was what caused his injuries, it's hardly surprising that his mind's gone blank.'

Emma's set had been given a week off in order to study for their final and most important examinations. Most nurses lived too far away to go home for that length of time and so they would have to hole up in their rooms in the Nurses' Home.

'You must come back with us, dear,' Rose said. 'It will do you good to get some country air and good home cooking.'

'But Pierce . . . '

'He'll be well looked after here,' Will said. 'Besides, you can bring the boy's school books back with you when you return and he can catch up with his studies. It will give him something to do while he's laid up. If I could afford it I'd hire a tutor to come in a couple of times a week, but he's already spent what I'd set aside for that purpose, and see where it's got him!'

'Don't keep harping on the subject, Will,' his wife told him. 'But you will come home, won't you, Emma? It would be lovely to have you at home again, if only for a while.'

So Emma travelled home by train with her parents, more than happy with the idea of a break. By the middle of the week she was heartily fed up with reviewing her nursing notes.

'Why not go out for a nice walk, dear?' Rose suggested. 'If you like you can go up to the farm. I've been baking, and no doubt Aunt Lizzie would welcome a few flapjacks.'

Emma was surprised to catch sight of Adam Abbot, coming along the road in her direction. 'Emma! I was just coming to call on you,' he said.

'Were you? What are you doing away from home at this time of day?'

'Lucy doesn't seem to know when you are heading back to the hospital, again and I wanted to make sure that I didn't miss you before you left.' They walked along in companionable silence for a while. They had been friends all their lives and there was no need for any awkwardness between them.

But that changed in the blink of an eye. 'Look here, Emma,' Adam said. 'There's something I want to ask you.'

'If you want me to take something back for Uncle Seth, of course I will.'

'It's not that.'

'So what is it, then?'

'We've always got on well, haven't we, the pair of us?'

'Of course we have, if you don't count that phase you went through when you used to lie in wait for me all over the place, giving me the fright of my life by jumping out at me, screeching like a wild animal.'

'That was a long time ago. What I mean is, don't you think we could make a go of it together? You like country life well enough, and I'll inherit the farm one of these days.'

'Not for a long time yet, I hope.' It was beginning to dawn on Emma that this was shaping up to be a proposal of marriage. 'What are you trying to say, Adam?'

'Isn't it obvious? I'm asking you to marry me, Emma.'

'Oh, dear! I don't know what to say.'

'I was hoping you'd say yes. I've missed you since you left Hartscombe and I realise that I want to spend the rest of my life with you.'

'This has come quite out of the blue, Adam. Marriage is a very serious commitment. I'm so sorry, but I'm not in love with you. I've hardly seen anything of you since I went to St Bee's. I'm sure we've both changed since we were children.'

Adam was quite red in the face now. 'I haven't changed, Emma. I haven't spoken sooner because I thought it best to give you your head when it came to this nursing business, but surely you've got it out of your system now? You've spent three years working like a galley slave for no pay, and it's time to come home. I'm willing to give you your head until you sit your exams, but then we can plan our wedding. I've spoken to Mum, and she's all in favour.'

'Give me my head, Adam? I'm not a horse! And as for 'letting' me have my career, I'm my own person. If my father allowed me to go to St Bee's, then nobody else has anything to say about it.'

'So it's no, then?'

'I'm afraid so, Adam.'

'I suppose you've got some fancy doctor in your sights! A mere farmer isn't good enough for you! Aunt Rose did mention something of the sort to Mum, as a matter of fact. That's why I made up my mind to speak to you, before he pipped me at the post.'

'All I have in my sights at the moment is the exams waiting for me next week!' Emma told him. 'Thank you for asking me, Adam. Believe me, I do appreciate it very much, but you must see that it wouldn't be any good.'

'I suppose that's that, then.' He turned on his heel and walked off in the direction of home. Emma found that she was still holding the flapjacks. She was about to call to him to wait, but she realised that he'd think she'd had second thoughts and would come bounding back, like a happy dog carrying a stick. What could she say to him then; here's a consolation prize? She, too, turned for home.

'You haven't been gone long,' Rose said, when her daughter entered the house. 'And what's that you're holding? Don't tell me you forgot to deliver my flapjacks, after all the trouble I went to!'

'Oh, Mum!'

'Why, what's the matter?'

'I met Adam in the lane.'

'And you didn't think to give them to him?'

'Oh, bother the flapjacks!' Emma cried.

'There's no need to speak to your mother like that, my girl!' Will said, frowning as Emma ran from the room.

'I expect she's upset, doing all that studying on top of worrying about Pierce. And perhaps Adam has said something to upset her even more.' A little smile hovered on Rose's lips as she looked at her husband's angry face. 'Don't look so cross dear. When I saw Lizzie at the shop the other day she let slip that Adam was screwing up the courage to propose to Emma.'

'Propose? Do you mean marriage?'

'Of course that's what I mean.'

'Bless my soul. Well, I must say I approve of the idea, don't you, love? He'd make an ideal husband.'

'Except that by the look of things our daughter doesn't fancy the idea. I did hint to Lizzie that there might be someone else in the offing, and perhaps that's what's brought him to the point.'

'That doctor? Do you think there's anything in that?'

'He certainly seemed interested. I'm not sure if his feelings are reciprocated, though. We shall have to wait and see.'

★ ★ ★

Upstairs, Emma was feeling rather shaken. If she was honest, she had turned Adam down because she had a glimmer of hope concerning James. Surely his kindness towards her parents and his interest in the progress of Pierce, who wasn't even his patient, meant something?

If she had never met James, would

she now be considering Adam's proposal? *No!* she told herself sternly, she would not. It hadn't been romantic in the least; thrown at her in the middle of a dusty country lane! And had he actually said anything about love? He had missed her, yes, but you could miss a friend, or a cat, even. There had to be more to marriage than that! And he'd been scathing about her nursing career as if it was some sort of girlish whim instead of a true vocation. As for saying he'd be 'willing' to let her sit her exams, just who did he think he was? If he was behaving like a Victorian husband now, what would it be like to spend the rest of her life with him? No, she had had a narrow escape there.

When her indignation had died down, she began to feel sorry for Adam. Had she said anything really hurtful to the poor man? She could not remember. His declaration had come as a shock to her and unkind things might have been said in the heat of the moment.

Knowing Adam as she did, she had no doubt that he wouldn't take no for an answer. He was quite likely to turn up on her doorstep again, this time with a bunch of flowers in his hand. Aunt Lizzie would probably give him a few hints as to how a suitor should behave!

It was a nuisance, but it might be best if she returned to St Bee's at once where she would be out of his reach. And, who knew, she might just happen to run into Dr James Townsend — quite by accident, of course!

* * *

Her exams over, Emma was able to go about her work with a light heart. Her brother was recovering nicely and it was only a matter of time before his leg healed and he was able to go home.

'I've had a letter from Mum,' he told her, when she dropped in to see him during her off duty hours.

'Is there any message for me?'

'Not exactly, but I s'pose she thinks

I'll tell you what's in the letter. Emma, there's something awful going on in Hartscombe!'

'There's not somebody stealing the washing off people's lines again?'

'Worse than that! There's men getting white feathers in the post. You know, when somebody thinks they're cowards for not joining up.'

'Perhaps there are a few shirkers who need shaking up. If we want to win this war we must all play our part.'

'You don't understand, Emma! Dad's had one, and so's Adam, and lots more chaps besides.'

'What! But who would give Dad a white feather? He's too old to start with and somebody has to keep the school running. As for Adam, he's a farmer. Who's going to feed the country if they send all the farmers to war? Whoever is doing this must be mad if they think that Aunt Lizzie can run the place single-handedly with only our Lucy to help her!'

'Mum says that Dad's very upset,

and he's talking about trying to enlist.'

Emma groaned. As if they hadn't had enough trouble already, with Pierce trying to learn to fly so he could go off to join the Flying Corps. Full marks to him for wanting to do his bit, of course, even if he was misguided, but as a schoolboy he'd be more of a hindrance than a help.

A thought struck her. 'I wonder why the feathers are coming in the post? I've heard of women coming up to men in the street and handing them a feather, but this seems odd. I suppose Dad knows whoever it is doing this. Well, I can't stop chatting here all day. I have to go and see Matron. If you're writing back to Mum, give her my love.'

'In trouble, are you?' Pierce grinned. He knew that everyone lived in dread of the formidable Matron.

'Cheeky! She wants to see all of our set. I expect it has something to do with what we'll do next if we've passed our exams.'

'You'll be going to France, won't you,

Emma? I wish I was going with you.'
Pierce looked so mournful that she had
to laugh. But any thoughts that she
might have had about going off to war
were doomed to disappointment when
Matron outlined her plans for her
immediate future.

'I should like to offer you a position
of Staff Nurse here at St Botolph's,'
Matron began. 'This, of course, is
contingent upon your being successful
in your examinations, which I'm sure
you will have done.'

'Thank you, Matron.'

'If you accept the post, I should like
to have your assurance that you will
remain here for at least a year. So many
of my nurses have gone to serve abroad
and my hospital simply cannot function
with probationers alone. Have you had
any intention of signing on to go to
France?'

'No, Matron.'

'Good. Then I take it that you will
accept my offer?'

'Yes, Matron. Thank you, Matron.'

At lunch time, Emma sought out Jenny, who was sitting at the table reserved for third year students, poking suspiciously at a fishcake.

'Do you suppose they actually put real fish in these things?' she demanded, as Emma slid into the seat beside her.

'Never mind that. Have you been to Matron yet?'

'Yes, and I'm going to London. I'm being transferred to a centre where they train girls as VADs — you know, to go over to France with the Voluntary Aid Detachment. What about you?'

'I'm staying on as a Staff Nurse.'

'I thought you'd be dashing off to volunteer to go to France. James is leaving soon, isn't he? I could just see the pair of you, working together in some hospital tent, saving lives and drinking tea out of tin mugs.'

'All at the same time?'

'Seriously, how are things between you and our handsome doctor?'

Emma shrugged. James certainly seemed interested in her and many a little friendly chat had taken place in odd corners of the hospital, when he had enquired after her parents or asked her how her studying was going. They had even had coffee together once or twice when they'd happened to run into each other in the town. But there had been no trips to the theatre, no romantic interludes when their hands had touched, or his lips had brushed her hair. All in all their relationship — if you could call it that — had been a bit of a disappointment.

She said as much to her friend, who replied, 'Well, what did you expect? You know how Matron frowns on relation-ships between doctors and trainee nurses. He probably doesn't want to land you in trouble. It will be different once we've qualified, just you wait and see.'

'By that time he'll be off to France. I was hoping we'd get somewhere before that happens, but it doesn't look as if it will.'

'Ah, but don't forget the hospital ball.'

'As if I could! I've looked at the notice board — I'm on duty that evening.'

'Can't you switch with someone?'

'I don't like to. That would mean someone else missing the ball.'

'I'm on duty myself, or I'd volunteer.'

'Aren't we a couple of Cinderellas! What we need is a fairy godmother!'

★ ★ ★

In the end it was Matron, of all people, who solved the problem. She issued a directive suggesting that any nurse who was able to attend the ball at the start should go back on the wards after two hours had elapsed, to give the unlucky ones a chance to take part. Each ward Sister was to make the arrangement ahead of time. Furthermore, students were to come to the ball in uniform.

'After all,' she concluded, 'there is a war on.'

This last comment caused some disappointment among those who had already purchased a new frock for the occasion. However, it was understood that they could hardly go back on duty in all their glory, so this way was fair to all. They would have to leave it to the senior staff to trip the light fantastic in all colours of the rainbow.

Emma was in a fine state of nerves by the time the great day arrived. 'I don't know if I'll go after all,' she told Jenny. 'Not coming straight off the ward, reeking of disinfectant. What if James doesn't ask me to dance? I'll die of embarrassment.'

Jenny laughed. 'This is a hospital, not the Ritz. Do you think you'll be the only one not smelling like a rose? Stop fretting and just enjoy yourself.'

So Emma went to the ball, which was held in the hospital boardroom in which the tables had been pushed back against the wall.

There was no sign of James. Perhaps the doctors, too, had agreed to fill in for others of their ilk, such as those who had to be on duty in Casualty.

However, a rather spotty medical student claimed her at once, and swung her into the dance. After him came a skinny youth who had just started work as a hospital porter. He confided that his friends had dared him to ask her to dance, and he had done so 'Just to show them'.

Amused, she asked, 'Should I take that as a compliment?' but the music was loud and he didn't hear. Finally he steered her to the refreshment table, where there was a choice between ginger beer and dandelion and burdock. She felt a tap on her shoulder.

'James! I didn't know if you were coming.'

'I couldn't miss this. I hope the next one is a waltz, because I don't think I can manage anything else.'

She was in his arms at last. She had

dreamed about this moment for such a long time, and she was dismayed when another medical student tried to cut in. 'On your way, sonny!' James said, grinning to take the sting out of the rejection.

'I say, that isn't fair!'

'Doctor's perks!' He steered Emma towards the French window, which was open to let in the night air.

'Where are we going?' she hissed. 'I'll be in trouble if Matron spots us!'

'She's too busy chatting up Sir Reginald Bellamy to notice a thing. Just look the other way and don't catch anyone's eye, that's all.'

Outside, in the shadow of a pillar, he drew her close to him. 'All these weeks, and we haven't been able to get a moment alone. Well, I intend to put that right this time.'

His kiss was so sweet that she almost gasped with the joy of it. He drew his head back and looked at her for a long moment, as if assessing her reaction. Trembling, she gave him a tentative smile and he leaned forward to kiss her again.

This time they did not draw apart for a long time, during which Emma felt that the world might well have stopped turning for all that she knew of what was happening inside the boardroom.

7

Lucy noticed that Adam was not his usual, cheerful self. He went about his work with a glum expression on his face, and he no longer joked or whistled. 'You shouldn't worry about that silly white feather,' she told him. 'Anybody with a grain of sense would know that you can't leave here. What would be the point of you going off to get yourself killed and leaving no one to run the farm? Don't let them force you to do something silly.'

'Oh, I'm not worried about that, Lucy. It's just some silly woman who should know better.'

'But it must be someone from Hartscombe, someone we know. All the men are getting them in the post, even Dad.'

'My dad as well. Though what they think he could do in the army, I just don't know, stuck in that hospital bed, barely able to move.'

'There you are, then. Don't let it bother you. I don't like to see you so unhappy. Isn't there something I can do?'

'Not unless you speak to your sister and get her to reconsider.'

'Reconsider? What do you mean?'

'I asked her to marry me, Lucy, and she turned me down flat. Do you think there might be a chance for me, Lucy? With Emma, I mean.'

Lucy felt a surge of love welling up in her breast. She loved Adam with all her heart. How could he not realise that? And how could he not know the hurt he was causing by telling her he meant to wed her sister?

'Mum thinks she might be going to marry a doctor, Adam.'

'That's just what I'm afraid of.'

'So you see, p'raps you shouldn't keep hoping. It wouldn't do any good.'

He put his head in his hands and gave a little hiccup that sounded suspiciously like a sob. Lucy put an arm around his shoulders. 'I love you, Adam, so awfully much.'

'That's nice,' he muttered.

'No, truly. If you asked me to marry you, I'd say yes in a second.'

'Don't be silly, Lucy, you're just a child.'

'I'm sixteen. Girls are married at sixteen, you know that.'

'So is this supposed to comfort me, Lucy Meadows? The woman I love turns me down, but that's all right, I can marry her baby sister instead and be reminded every day of my life of what I've lost? You're talking utter rot!' He stood up abruptly and left her, red-faced and chagrined, leaning against the stone wall. It was some time before she was able to pull herself together and go into the house.

'Where on earth have you been, child?' Lizzie demanded, pushing back wisps of hair that had escaped from her turban. 'I wanted you to help me turn the mattresses but you were nowhere to be found. If you've ever tried flipping a feather bed on your own, you'll know just how difficult it is.' She peered at Lucy, whose eyes were red-rimmed. 'What's the matter with you? Have you been crying?'

'It's Adam. He was horrid to me, Aunt Lizzie. Positively brutal!'

'Oh? And what did you do to make him turn on you? That doesn't sound like our Adam.'

'He's just so unhappy because Emma turned him down, and he got cross when I offered to marry him instead.'

'What?'

'There's no need for you to shout at me as well, Aunt Lizzie.'

'Let me get this straight. You went up to Adam and proposed marriage to him, and you a silly chit of fifteen. What on earth were you playing at, child? Haven't we enough to worry about without you playing silly games?'

'It wasn't a game, Aunt Lizzie, and I'm sixteen now. Juliet was only fourteen when she fell in love with Romeo.'

'Yes, and look what happened to her. But never mind them. What on earth possessed you to behave as you did?'

'Adam told me he was hurt because Emma turned him down. I told him it'll do him no good to keep hoping she'll come round, because Mum thinks she may marry that doctor from her hospital. Then I told him I'd marry him.'

'Lucy Meadows, I'm flabbergasted.'

'But what was wrong with that? I love him, and I like working here on the farm. I'd make him a good wife, I know I would.'

'Now you listen to me, my girl! To begin with, no decent woman proposes to a man, she waits to be asked! This may be 1915 but some things never change. Poor old Queen Victoria would turn in her grave to hear you talking like this. You should be ashamed! Seems to me I should have a word with your father, my girl! Maybe he can set you straight!'

'Oh, please don't say anything to Dad!'

'And you give me one good reason why I shouldn't. You've been spoiled, Lucy Meadows, that's your trouble. Your Mum's been treating you with kid gloves ever since you were ailing as a kiddie. Well, those days are long gone, and it's time you learned to see sense. Now you run along home and let me get on with my work.'

Lucy fled, the tears rolling down her crimson cheeks. Snatching up her bicycle she pedalled down the lane with her legs going like pistons.

How could she ever face Aunt Lizzie again, to say nothing of Adam? And what if the beastly woman made good her promise to report their conversation to Dad? Lucy could imagine what he'd have to say and he was not in the best of tempers these days, what with one thing and another.

By the time she reached home a plan had formed in her mind, and when she came to the house and found that nobody was there, she knew what she had to do. Throwing a few garments into a battered holdall she took down her piggy bank and inserted a knife into the slot. She soon had a small pile of coins, which she hoped would cover the one-way fare to London.

If she hurried, she could catch the five o'clock train.

★ ★ ★

Will and his wife arrived home at the same time. Rose had been to her Red Cross meeting, and he had been delayed in the school, trying to sort out a problem to do with some missing slates.

'Is Lucy not in yet?' he asked.

'I don't think so. I expect she's still up at the farm. I do hope they're not working the child too hard. I've warned Lizzie how delicate she is.'

'You worry too much, Rose. I'm sure it's doing her good, working in the fresh air and sunshine. Much better than staying cooped up in her room with all those novelettes she's so fond of reading.'

He went off to his study, only to turn back again when he heard an agonised shriek coming from the kitchen. 'Rose! Are you all right?'

'Look what I found, propped up against the tea caddy!'

Will snatched the note from her, and read it aloud, as if she didn't already know what it contained. 'I have gone to London to be a VAD. Don't worry about me. Love, Lucy.' He peered at it, disbelieving the words in front of his eyes. He read it again, and then a third time.

'Why has she done this?' Rose wailed. 'Oh, my poor baby! We've got to stop her, Will! Get down to the station and stop her, before it's too late!'

'I'm afraid it's already too late. I heard the train whistle when I was crossing the playground. The train has gone. There's nothing we can do.'

'But to be alone in London at her

age! She won't know where to go or what to do! And they won't take her on as a VAD; she's too young.'

'Then they'll just send her home again, I expect.'

'But she can't have had much money, Will. How will she manage? And London will be full of rough soldiers, anything could happen to her — and I've heard of white slavers being on the lookout for young girls on their own! Oh, Will, what are we going to do?'

He shook his head, having no words of comfort for his poor wife. He would contact the authorities, of course, ask them to look out for a young girl arriving on the train from Gloucestershire, but the chances of Lucy being spotted were slim. The station was likely to be full of troop trains, disgorging wounded men sent home from the front. One slender young girl would be swallowed up in the crowd.

Meanwhile, sitting in a third class carriage, being jolted from side to side, Lucy was beginning to regret her hasty flight. Having had no tea she was beginning to feel pangs of hunger. If only she had made a sandwich to bring with her. And she had no fixed plan of how to proceed when she arrived in London. Well, she had a tongue in her head, and she could ask for directions. She would find some respectable-looking matron and ask her where she should go.

8

For Emma, it was a time of change, mostly for the better. Since the night of the ball she had been going out with James on a regular basis. Not that their activities were romantic or terribly exciting, for they had little time to spare, or for that matter any money to spend on expensive outings. Nevertheless it was enough to be together, as they walked hand in hand through a nearby park.

She had also been successful in her examinations and was entitled to wear a frilly cap with bows to prove it.

'You look like a dear little cat,' James said fondly, fingering the bows attached to her cap that were tied under her chin.

'The veil was a lot more comfortable,' she grumbled, but even so she was immensely proud of this new form of headgear, which proclaimed her a fully-fledged Staff Nurse.

'You must have your photograph taken, Emma. I'm sure your parents will want a copy and I certainly want a little one to take to France with me.'

'Do you, James?'

'Of course I do. I shall gaze at it while I'm writing my letters to you, or when I'm waiting for the letters I hope you are going to send to me.'

Emma smiled rather sadly. She was thrilled to have matters settled between them at last, but if only he didn't have to go to war!

'It'll be all right, Emma. Surely this war can't last much longer, and then I'll come marching home again. I don't want to commit you to anything now, just in case something happens to me, but when it's all over I'll have an important question to ask you.'

She began to speak, to assure him that, no matter what dangers lay ahead, she was ready to make a commitment now, but he gently placed a finger on her lips to stop her from speaking.

She so much wished that she had his ring, no matter how inexpensive it might be. She could wear it on a string around her neck and feel it there, every minute of the day while he was away, but he must be feeling anxious about what the near future held for him. She would not put pressure on him.

* * *

She tried to explain this to Jenny, but her friend had other things on her mind. 'I wish now I hadn't said I'd go to this beastly place in London. I shan't know a soul there. And I hate the thought of having to preach to all these girls of my own age. I'm sure they won't listen to a word I say.'

'Preach? What on earth do you mean?'

'It's not just nursing technique, you know. They've sent me a pamphlet outlining what my responsibilities are and it seems I'm to be the guardian of their morals as well! If these VADS get to know our doctors over there, as they will, they are not to make a move in their off duty hours without a chaperone, even if that is only one of their own set. If they go out for a meal with a member of the opposite sex, they must take another girl along to play gooseberry. As for doing anything to disgrace the uniform, as this little book so quaintly puts it, they will be shipped home at once!'

'It doesn't sound very different from St Bee's, actually. Considering the ghastly hours we all work, I'd be very surprised if any nurse ever had the energy to get into mischief in her off duty hours.'

'Well, I'm all packed, and ready to fight the good fight. You will write to me, won't you, Emma? Tell me what it's like being a Staff Nurse — and of course you must let me know how James is getting on over there. Let me know about Pierce, too. Do you think he's given up on the Flying Corps?'

'I should think they'll have given up the idea of him, after he managed to demolish a biplane! We're still waiting to hear if Dad is expected to pay for the thing.'

★ ★ ★

James went away, and so did Jenny. Emma was glad that her brother was still in the hospital because that meant she had someone belonging to her to go and visit.

When she next went to his ward she found him in an excitable state.

'Here's a letter from Mum. It's addressed to both of us, so you'd better read it. She says Lucy's run away to France, to be some sort of nurse.'

'Give me that! If this is some sort of joke, I'll pull your nose!'

With growing horror Emma read the tear-stained letter which her mother had written on the morning after Lucy's disappearance.

I believe she must have had a

disagreement with Aunt Lizzie, but why run off like that? If she'd come to me we could have talked it through, whatever it was, and sorted it all out. I'm writing to you, Emma, in the hope that you may be able to do something through your nursing connections. Has Lucy ever discussed with you the idea of her going into nursing? You are the obvious person she'd turn to if she was thinking of a nursing career, and I suppose she wouldn't have mentioned it to me because I'd disapprove. Nursing is a fine career for you, dear, but not for poor delicate little Lucy.

'Delicate my foot!' Pierce grumbled, when Emma read this bit aloud. 'Strong as a horse is our Lucy, and well you know it.'

'Oh, my goodness, I do hope that this has nothing to do with me,' Emma murmured anxiously.

'Why? What have you done?'

'Nothing, really. It's just that Adam proposed to me and I turned him down. Perhaps that upset Aunt Lizzie and she's taken it out on Lucy.'

'Not enough to make the girl run away from home, surely?'

'Don't ask me. There is something I can do, though. Jenny Adams — you don't know her but she was my room mate until recently — has gone to London to help train girls as VADs. I'll write to her and tell her to keep a lookout for Lucy. Even if there's more than one recruiting centre there, Jenny should be able to let us know where they are. We'll soon have her safe and back home again.'

'Or if the worst happens, and she slips through the net, your Doctor Townsend will be able to track her down in France.'

'Heaven forbid she gets that far, Pierce. If there's any justice in the world she'll get stopped in her tracks as soon as she applies for training. Even I couldn't be sent to France unless I lied about my age. You have to be twenty-three, and Lucy is only just sixteen. As soon as they set eyes on her she'll be packed off home. Now I have things to do, so I want you to dash off a letter to Mum. Tell her what I've said to you, won't you? It may comfort her to know that I'm about to set the wheels in motion.'

Pierce made a gloomy face. 'If I know Mum, that won't stop her fretting. You know what a fusspot she is, especially where our Lucy's concerned.'

'Never mind that. Just do it, all right?'

When her letter was written and popped into the pillar box on the corner, which still bore the insignia of the late Queen Victoria, Emma heaved a sigh. If only James was still here, he might have been able to do more. He must have contacts in London and, since he had already gone through the process of signing up to go to France he would know all about it.

She wondered if she ought to speak to Matron about it. Could she even request compassionate leave so she could go and search for Lucy herself?

But no; she was a newly appointed Staff Nurse, not even eligible for holidays for ages. Matron would only tell her she couldn't be spared

Bother Lucy! If she could only get hold of her young sister right now she'd give her a good slap. How could the girl hurt their parents like this?

When Emma returned to the Nurses's Home she was waylaid by Home Sister. 'There you are, Nurse! I've been trying to find you. I've three letters for you that were put into the wrong pigeon hole by mistake. They were mixed up with Nurse Matthews' mail, but she's been at home in Wales for a few days and these only came to light on her return. I'm so sorry this happened, and I do hope that they're not anything important, or something that needed an immediate response.'

'Thank you, Sister.' Emma was delighted to see that all three letters were from France. Sister must have realised that, because she'd had to read the address in order to sort the post.

She must be consumed with curiosity, but Emma wasn't about to explain. She scuttled off, anxious to get to her room before she was stopped by anyone else.

James began by saying that he was well, but that he missed her. A good start! He went on to say that he was billeted in a bell tent along with other doctors. It was very damp and he felt cold all the time. He had been thrown in at the deep end, performing surgery at a casualty clearing station, only he wasn't allowed to tell her where that was, or the censors would black it out.

'I won't end by saying wish you were here,' he wrote, 'because this place is hell on earth and I wouldn't wish it on anybody. I think about you all the time, though, especially when I fall asleep on my rickety old camp bed. I can't wait for my first leave, when I'll be able to come back and see you again. All my love, James.'

All three letters contained much the same sort of thing, because there wasn't much else to say. To Emma they meant the world, for James had sent her all his love. He wasn't the most articulate of men speaking face to face, but obviously he could express himself better on paper.

'Just keep those letters coming, my love,' she whispered, as if her thoughts could wing their way to France to be intercepted by him. She must write to him immediately and try to produce some words of love to equal his.

★ ★ ★

When Lucy stepped down from the train, she gazed about her in utter bewilderment. She found herself in a huge cavern of a place that echoed with barely comprehensible announcements coming from a loudspeaker. People were hurrying here and there, mingling with what seemed to be the whole British army, waiting for trains.

She felt in her pocket where a very few coins jingled. She longed for something to eat, but decided she'd better not spend the money she had left in case she had to travel on a horse omnibus to reach her destination.

The first thing to do was to make enquiries as to where that place might be. She noticed a kiosk with the word *Information* written over the door, but it was surely two platforms away and she had no idea at all how to reach it.

This was all so new to her. She had never been out of Hartscombe before, except for the annual Sunday School treat, when the children were taken in a hay wagon to a farmer's field, where they had races and ate buns. Still, sitting meekly with her hands folded had never been Lucy's way. She could handle this.

She went up to a woman who was dispensing mugs of cocoa to soldiers. Pausing in her task, the woman stared at her as if she'd gone mad.

'The recruiting centre — at this time of night? They won't be open now. I can certainly direct you, but there's no point in your going there before tomorrow morning, unless you want to sleep on the steps.'

'But what am I to do?'

'I suggest you go to the YWCA — the Young Women's Christian Association — and get some supper and a bed for the night.'

'Will I have to pay?'

'Why, of course you will. They're not a charity.'

'But I don't have any money. At least, just a few coppers.'

'Then you are in a pickle, aren't you? Look, have a cup of cocoa; it's free. Then go and find a bench and stay there for the night. Most of these men will be leaving soon and you'll be able to find a space. Do not talk to anyone, unless it's somebody in the uniform of the Salvation Army, and most of all, do not go with anyone who offers you a place to stay, or who promises to conduct you to the recruiting hospital. That goes for women as well as men. Do I make myself plain?'

'I think so, and thank you for the cocoa.'

'That's all right, and please return the mug when it's empty.'

Lucy sat on a nearby luggage trolley, sipping the cocoa slowly, trying to make it last. She couldn't help hearing what the canteen woman was saying to her companion, and the words caused her to flush with embarrassment.

'Another runaway girl, by the look of it.'

'Did she say where she's going?'

'She says she's come to sign on as a VAD.'

'She'll be lucky! You have to be at least twenty-one, even for home service, and she doesn't look more than fourteen.'

'These girls and their romantic ideas of smoothing the fevered brows of wounded men! If she could see some of the sights I've seen, those poor souls being carried off the hospital trains, she'd have a fit of the vapours, I don't doubt.'

'Do you think we ought to do something about her? Have a word with the station police, perhaps? She's far too young to be wandering about here unsupervised. Anything might happen to her.'

'No, no. Let the proper authorities see to her. When she tells her story to them at the hospital they'll soon send her packing. Brace yourself, Connie! Here comes another train, and the other urn isn't hot enough yet.'

Strangely, these words buoyed Lucy up. So these women thought she was too young and silly to cope, did they? She'd show them!

* * *

The next morning, stiff and sore after a night on a hard bench, she went to a ladies' convenience and tidied herself up as best she could. She was then given directions by a portly man in a rumpled uniform who had the information down pat.

Her stomach rumbled as she made her way to the exit where a number of omnibuses were drawn up. Finding the one she wanted she clambered aboard and sat back to take in her surroundings from the vantage point of an open-air upper deck.

The conductress warned her when they were coming to her stop and she clattered down the stairs and hopped down onto the pavement, filled with excitement. Within minutes she was at the hospital, being directed to a hall where three uniformed women were seated at tables, interviewing would-be nurses.

The minutes ticked by until, finally, it was Lucy's turn.

'How old are you?'

'Um, twenty-one.'

'Oh, yes?' The woman sniffed her disbelief. 'Can we see your birth certificate, then?'

'I haven't got one. At least, I suppose I have, but I didn't bring it with me.'

'Then you'll have to go home and fetch it. Next!'

'But I can't go home, Miss. I've come all the way from Gloucestershire and I only had a one-way ticket. I haven't got any more money left, and I'm so hungry!'

'There's no need to wail like that, girl! Go and sit down and I'll send someone to fetch you a cup of tea. After that you can go and see the almoner. She'll have to deal with you, because I certainly can't. Just look at that queue, and the morning isn't over yet. Well, what are you waiting for? Do as you're told girl and go and sit down.'

The almoner was a thin, harassed woman who dealt with Lucy kindly. 'If only you girls would make the proper enquiries before you come haring down to London,' she sighed. 'How old are you really? Fifteen? Sixteen?'

'Sixteen,' Lucy admitted.

'What on earth were you thinking of, trying to get taken on as a VAD?'

'My sister is a nurse, and I've heard her say that some hospitals do take on girls of my age.'

'To begin training as nursery nurses, perhaps, but not to join the Voluntary Aid Detachment! Didn't your sister tell you you'd have to be twenty-one, even to work in a military hospital in England? To go to France a young woman has to meet even more stringent requirements, being twenty-three with at least three month's hospital experience.'

'I haven't seen her lately.'

'The question now is, what are we going to do about you. Are you sure you don't have enough money for your fare home?'

Lucy turned out her pocket, revealing a threepenny bit, three ha'pennies and a farthing.'

'Oh, dear! That won't take you far.'

'Couldn't I borrow some? I'm sure my father would send you a postal order to repay it.'

'I expect he would, but you see the hospital has no funds for that sort of thing. I do have one suggestion, though. We are desperately short of maids here.

So many have left to work in munitions factories. Would you like to sign on for that? You'll get a room here, plus all your meals and a weekly wage packet. You could do worse.'

A maid! Lucy thought of Cherry, who had worked in their house since the age of twelve. Lucy had taken her presence for granted and had often added to the girl's work by failing to make her own bed or tidy her room.

'What would I have to do?'

'Your work would entail much the same things as the probationer VADs are required to do. Sweeping and dusting in the wards, cleaning patients' lockers, doing the washing up and other kitchen duties, scouring sinks and bedpans, and sorting dirty linen.'

Lucy gulped. 'All right, I'll do it.'

Relieved, the almoner stood up. 'Come along, then. I'll take you to see the housekeeper. She'll give you a contract to sign, and you'll be issued with a uniform. We're so short-handed, I expect you'll be asked to start right away. And just be grateful you're not being taken on as VAD, for they have to provide their own uniforms, and those cost money!'

The housekeeper was a formidable woman in a green serge uniform. Fumbling in a drawer she whipped out a sheaf of papers which she commanded Lucy to sign.

'You'd better start her off for just three months,' the almoner warned. 'If she settles down she can always renew later. Now I must be off. I have a list of people a yard long to see today. Oh, and before I forget, she's had nothing to eat for twenty-four hours. She'd better be fed before she starts work, or you won't get much out of her.'

*　*　*

Lucy soon found herself in a long dining hall which, at this time of day, was empty except for two small maids who were busy scrubbing tables. 'That'll be me tomorrow,' she told herself, as she attacked the doorsteps of bread, accompanied by a scraping of plum jam. Things were looking up. She actually had a job. Having left the security of a home where she was treated like a child she had come out into the world and immediately landed herself a job and a place to stay. All she had to do now was to prove herself, and all would be well. It did not occur to her that she should write to inform her suffering parents of this fact.

9

Will Meadows was at his desk with his head in his hands. He had left his wife sobbing at the kitchen table, begging him to find Lucy. But what could he do? He had a school to run and he couldn't just leave Miss Fiske and Miss Landers to cope alone, especially since he was responsible for teaching the top class himself. Even if he could go, where would he start? London was a big place.

'There can't be that many hospitals in London, Will. All you'd have to do is stop at each one and ask if Lucy is there. Would that be so difficult? If you won't go, I shall. I won't sleep until Lucy is safely back home here with us.'

Will shuddered to think of his wife on the loose in the big city. She had been anxious enough travelling to Gloucester, and he had accompanied her then. But he knew that she would tackle anything, no matter how stressful, if it meant bringing her daughter home.

'Please say you'll go, Will. If you love me, you'll do it.'

'That's a low blow, Rose. And believe me, I want the girl home as much as you do, but we have to go about this sensibly. I've already had a word with the constable, and he has promised to telegraph Scotland Yard. We should hear back today, and after that we'll sit down and talk about what to do next. Will you wait until then, dear?'

Reluctantly, his wife agreed to do nothing for the moment. 'But it's so hard to wait, Will. Can't you see that?'

He could, only too well. Sitting alone in the silent classroom. Waiting for the school day to begin, he thought about his life. He had tried so hard to do the right thing always, so where had he gone wrong?

How could he hope to instill right thinking into the minds of his young charges, when he had lost control of his own family? His son was now lying in a hospital bed and his youngest daughter had run away from home.

Now he had to solve the mystery of the missing slates before the pupils arrived for the day. He suspected that their disappearance had something to do with Bessie Baxter, a young girl in Miss Fiske's class. She was so lacking in self confidence that he had appointed her as a monitor, thinking that the little honour would do her the world of good. He and Miss Fiske would share the child's services, which included cleaning the blackboard, washing out dusters, filling ink wells and doing general tidying.

The slates were an important part of school life. The younger children used them for all their written work, while the seniors used them for mathematics. They had copy books in which they practiced their copperplate handwriting.

Miss Fiske had not yet arrived when

Will entered her classroom. Opening the map cupboard, he was pleased to find a pile of slates on a lower shelf, but noticed an envelope at the back of the shelf, several white feathers protruding from the flap. He pulled the package out, his heart thumping.

'Oh!' Miss Fiske arrived unheard, padding in on her soft house shoes.

'Good morning, Miss Fiske. I've found the slates. Bessie must have thought she was meant to tidy them away. But while I was at it I came across these feathers. Can you explain what they are doing here?'

He waited, hoping that it had something to do with the child. Had she been distributing the white feathers as a sort of game? But that was hardly likely, for they had come through the post. A child of her age could not afford to buy the necessary stamps, nor would she know how to address the envelopes properly.

Miss Fiske broke down. 'I didn't mean any harm,' she sobbed.

'You didn't mean any harm? Speaking for myself, you caused me great distress, and what about poor Seth Abbot, lying in his hospital bed?'

'I know! I know! I can't think what came over me.'

'But why? You must know why you did it.'

'Well, my sister had just received a marconigram to say that her son was killed over there. Young Alfie, her only child. He was such a pet as a little boy. He used to come to stay with me and he gladdened my heart with his childish prattle. Such a sunny little chap, he was. Now I'll never see him again, and I can't bear it, Mr Meadows!'

'So you thought you'd shame a few more of us into getting ourselves killed, eh? Was that supposed to make you feel better?'

'I happen to feel that if our army was a great deal bigger we could defeat that Kaiser all the sooner. And I've heard that the government is going to bring in conscription soon, so all the shirkers won't have a leg to stand on.'

'So despite my age, and the essential job I'm doing here, you hope they'll send me off to war, Miss Fiske?'

She tossed her head in defiance. 'Perhaps you couldn't do much to help, but I didn't care for the way you treated your poor boy when he was doing his best to train as a fighting man — a fat lot of support he got from you.'

'I hate to have to say this about my own son, but he stole money to pay for those flying lessons, and I cannot condone that.'

'Is that what you think? You'll find that money safe in his room.'

'Then where did he get the money from? He receives a very small amount of pocket money.'

'I gave it to him, Mr Meadows. That's what paid for his flying lessons. That money came from me.'

'What are you trying to tell me, Miss Fiske?

'I believe I'm speaking plainly enough. We were having a chat after school one day and he told me that it was his dream to fly. He'd been to the aerodrome and been taken on a flight, but it had wiped out all his savings. He could only go back for the lessons he needed if he could raise the money somehow. Nothing was said about the possibility of misappropriating the money you'd given him to pay for his tutoring. I had some money I'd been saving up for Alfie so that he could get started in an apprenticeship. Then he was killed, so I gave it to Pierce. He was a favourite of mine, you know.'

Will hardly knew what to say. Finally he murmured something about flying being a dangerous occupation.

'So is living in a muddy trench and getting shot at by the enemy! Is that what you want for Pierce? And think of all those other lads, boys whose names you read out at morning assembly with tears in your eyes! No, I'm not sorry I did what I did. Rose will have me to thank when her boy comes home to her, safe, if not sound.'

'The constable will have to be told that you were behind this white feather business, you know.'

'See if I care!' the teacher said. 'I'm a woman of principle!'

'I have to step across to the house for a minute or two,' Will said at last. 'When the time comes you may ring the bell, then you can supervise the lines and march the children in. If I'm not back in time, you will have to take prayers. I've placed a bookmark in the testament, so you'll be able to find the reading for today.'

Miss Fiske inclined her head in dignified agreement with his words.

Will went straight to Pierce's room and began to search the most likely hiding places. Tipping up the mattress he found a small leather wallet, which he recognised as one that had belonged to the boy's grandfather. The amount of money inside tallied exactly with that which he had set aside for the boy's tutoring.

'Is that you, Will? Who is up there?

What are you doing?' Rose rushed up the stairs, brandishing the poker.

'Put that down, love, before you do yourself an injury.'

'Shouldn't you be in school? And why is that bed in such a muddle?'

Will held out the money to his wife, who frowned, puzzled now. 'It's all the money I gave Pierce to pay old Butler. He didn't steal it after all,' he told her bluntly.

'Then where did he get the money to go flying with?'

Will told his wife what he knew.

'Old Miss Fiske! How extraordinary! Well, I'm glad that this has come to light. And what ought you to do about that white feather business? Surely you don't want to make it a police matter? It's our Red Cross meeting his afternoon. Why don't I have a word with all the women there and ask them to put out the word discreetly in the village? I suspect that they'll under-stand what made her do it and she'll be forgiven. Most of us have either lost someone to this beastly war, or know people who have.'

So Will returned to the school with a lighter heart, and Rose was glad to have a bit of better news to spread about. 'Now, if only we could find our Lucy, I'd be a happy woman,' she said to Lizzie Abbot. 'I don't suppose you have any idea of what made her rush off like that?'

'It wasn't my fault!' Truth to tell, Lizzie had been feeling guilty about the home truths she'd inflicted on Lucy, who was only a silly child, after all.

'Nobody said that it was. What are you talking about?'

'Well, I might have been a bit harsh with the girl, I suppose, but probably Adam was just as offhand.'

'What on earth did the girl do to upset the pair of you?'

'She asked Adam to marry her!' Lizzie said. Rose gasped in disbelief.

* * *

In January, 1916, conscription was introduced in Britain. All single, able-bodied men between the ages of eighteen and forty-one were to be called up for war service.

'That lets you out, Will,' his wife remarked, with great satisfaction.

In due course the plan was expanded to include married men as well, although by that time Will had reached his forty-second birthday. He half expected to receive papers in any case, but the weeks went by and nothing came. His neighbours were not so lucky. Both Seth and Adam were summoned to report to a training camp, much to Lizzie Abbot's dismay.

'You have to go to the doctor, Seth,' she insisted. It's about all you can do to put one foot in front of the other, let alone go on route marches!'

'There's nothing wrong with me, Mum,' Adam said. 'They'd have me in uniform in a heartbeat.'

'But what about the farm? What's going to happen here! First we lost

Peter — he was killed over there. Then your father was hurt and had to spend weeks in hospital. We did have Lucy for a bit, for all the good it did us, now she's run off to goodness knows where. What do they expect us to do; kill off all our milk cows? I'll have to speak to Mrs Fanshawe, that's what I'll do.'

'Who's she when she's at home?'

'Chairman of our Red Cross branch. Her husband's a magistrate. He'll tell us what we should do.'

Accordingly Lizzie called on this lady, who in turn spoke to her husband. 'Albert says you should tell your husband not to bother going to his own doctor. He'll be lost in a mass of red tape. Tell him to report to the nearest recruiting station, where doctors there will see him. They'll write him off as unfit. As for your son, he'll have to go before a tribunal to get an exemption.'

Accordingly Seth limped into a recruiting station and was rejected on sight. His son appeared before the tribunal where he was given a grilling.

'Are you a conscientious objector?' one of the magistrates sneered.

'I am nothing of the kind!' Adam snapped. 'I'm a farmer, that's what I am, and I want to know how we keep going if you send me off.'

'Have you no workers who can take your place?'

'We only had one man and he's gone off to France long since and been killed for his trouble. My dad's lame, my mother's overworked and if I'm taken away they'll be in a pretty pickle. Sirs, I want you to know that I'm fighting this war in my own way and there's nothing more I can do.'

The three men conferred. It was obvious from their expressions that one agreed with him, another was against him, and the third was in doubt. At last they came back to him. 'You have been given an exemption,' the friendly one assured him, stamping a bevy of forms which were handed to him as if it was a priceless treasure.

'Stupid bureaucrats!' Adam hissed, as

he passed another man who was waiting in line and then he was on his way home with the good news.

★ ★ ★

On the first of July a terrible battle began on the Somme, the area surrounding the Somme River in the Picardy region of France. The battle raged for more than two weeks with great loss of life in the British ranks.

'This says 58,000 dead,' Will mourned, glancing over his newspaper. 'And heaven knows how many more have been wounded or maimed for life. At this rate I wouldn't be surprised if they have to put up the age for forced enlistment, but don't ask me where they'll find the extra men. They'll be asking for children and retired chaps next.'

He could hardly bear to keep reading, and so it was that the name of Dr James Townsend in the casualty lists passed him by.

10

In London, however, it was with great sadness that Nurse Jenny Adams saw that Lieutenant James Townsend of the Royal Army Medical Corps had been killed in France.

'Oh, poor Emma,' she whispered. Not only that, but she had known and liked James herself. She wondered what had happened. Not that it mattered; the tragedy was that he had been killed.

Desperately wishing that there was something she could do to ease her friend's pain, she resolved to make a better effort to trace the errant little sister. She had received Emma's letter some time ago, asking her to be on the lookout for Lucy, but life had been so busy that she hadn't had a minute to spare. One thing was certain; Lucy would not have been accepted to train as a VAD, being only sixteen, so where could she be?

Unbeknown to Jenny, Lucy was in the very same hospital, hating every minute of it, but that was soon to change. Jenny was walking down a long corridor one morning when she heard the housekeeper scolding a small maid, who was scrubbing away at the floor but not making much progress.

'Do get a move on, Beddoes! You're supposed to be scrubbing that floor, not playing in a paddling pool. If you hope to keep working here, you'll have to do better than this!'

Jenny stopped suddenly. Beddoes? Or could that be Meadows? She bent over the unhappy girl, being careful not to topple the bucket of dirty water that lay between them.

'I say, are you by any chance Lucy Meadows?'

Lucy looked up at her. 'Yes, I am, actually. Who are you?'

'I'm Jenny Adams. I was Emma's roommate at St Bee's. Perhaps you've heard her mention me? I work here now. Look, you'd better get on. Miss Barton is staring at us. I'll come and find you later, shall I?'

Jenny immediately went to her office and dashed off a letter to Lucy's parents. Having sealed it and stamped it she placed it in the outgoing mail tray, knowing that it would be posted in time for the last collection of the day. Very likely the girl would beg Jenny not to notify her parents of her whereabouts, so by sending a letter before she met with Lucy she could not then be coerced into keeping quiet.

It was obvious from Emma's recent letter that the Meadows were in great distress over their youngest child's disappearance, as any parents would be, and they deserved to be relieved from their misery as soon as possible. Jenny had no compunction about letting the girl down in that regard.

As it turned out, though, when Jenny met with her later, the girl was in a state of abject misery, deeply regretting what she had done to herself. Unfortunately she appeared to have no remorse with regard to what she had put her parents through.

'I think you're a very silly little girl, Lucy. Do you have any idea what you've done to your parents? What on earth made you do this? I gather from what Emma has told me that you've never had the slightest interest in nursing, so what made you think of applying to be a VAD?'

'I wanted to show them,' the girl muttered.

'That sounds to me as if you wanted to get back at someone. Who was it, Lucy? Your parents?'

'Not them. The Abbots.'

'Ah, yes. Mr Abbot was on my ward at St Bee's. And I understand that his son — Adam, isn't it — asked Emma to marry him,' Jenny observed.

'Yes, and he was so distressed when she turned him down. I love Adam, and I wanted to make him feel better.'

'I see. And you had a falling out as a result?'

'It wasn't just him. It was his mother. She was absolutely beastly to me.'

'I still don't see why you had to run away. Couldn't you have let your mother sort out the problem, whatever it was?'

'I just couldn't face anybody. I was too embarrassed.'

Jenny was sure there must be more to this than Lucy was making out, but she decided not to probe further.

'I have to tell you something, Lucy. I've written to your parents, letting them know where you are.'

'You didn't! I hate you! How could you be so mean?'

'It's time you stopped thinking only about yourself, Lucy Meadows. Something very sad has happened to your sister, Emma, and your family doesn't need that on top of everything else. You have to make it up with your parents as soon as possible so they can find the strength to help your sister in her hour of need.'

Lucy's eyes opened wide. 'She hasn't

caught some nasty illness from one of the patients, has she? She isn't going to die, is she?'

'No, she isn't, but she might wish that she could.'

'I don't know what you mean.'

'A friend of hers — a doctor — has been killed in France. He was very dear to her, and I believe she hoped to marry him when this war is over. That is why you must do your part to draw your family together.'

★ ★ ★

When Emma was sent for by Matron, she didn't feel at all alarmed. As far as she knew she wasn't due for a wigging for everything was going well on the ward to which she had been recently assigned. In fact the Sister in charge had praised her for her leadership of the younger probationers.

'Come in.' Emma slipped inside Matron's office, closing the door behind her. 'Ah, Staff Nurse Meadows.

Do sit down. How are you feeling?'

'I'm very well, thank you, Matron.

'Then you haven't heard. Oh, dear. I'm afraid it's bad news, Nurse. Doctor Townsend has been killed in France.'

For a moment Emma couldn't take it in. Then she shook her head. 'That can't be true. I had two letters from him only this morning.'

'I'm afraid they must have been sent off just before. His name is here, in the casualty lists. I'm so sorry, Nurse.' Matron handed over a newspaper and there, ringed in red pencil, was James Townsend's name.

Emma felt her face growing stiff with the effort of trying to remain calm. One of Sister Tutor's often-heard maxims was 'always maintain a calm exterior'. She saw that Matron was watching her with a sympathetic expression on her face.

'Would you like some time off, Nurse, a few days' compassionate leave? Or would you prefer to keep on working? I know that grief affects people in differ-ent ways. Perhaps you'd like to go and visit his parents, who will have been informed of the sad news by now.'

'Thank you, Matron. I can't seem to think just now.' Emma's whole body felt numb, and she hoped she wasn't about to faint.

'Go along now and make yourself a cup of tea. Then come back and let me know what you've decided.'

'You're very kind, Matron.'

'Far be it from me to say I know how you must be feeling, but I do have some idea. It isn't generally known, but I lost a fiancé in the South African War. He was in the cavalry, the 10th Hussars, and died at Johannesburg.'

'I'm so sorry to hear that, Matron.'

'I'm afraid these things happen every day, when there's a war on.'

Emma stumbled along to the staff nurses' common room which, fortunately, was deserted at this time of day. While she waited for the kettle to boil she reflected on what she had just heard.

Matron had been almost human, not

at all like the usual starchy self she was used to. Perhaps she had managed to keep going by immersing herself in her work, and in the end that had helped her to rise to the top of her chosen career as matron of this great hospital. Would Emma do the same?

Suddenly she knew what she was going to do next. Turning off the gas under the kettle she hurried back to Matron's office.

'I've decided I'd like some compassionate leave, please. If I stay here at St Bee's where I used to catch a glimpse of James every day, I don't know if I could bear it.'

'I understand, Nurse. Very well. I can spare you for ten days. Go home to your parents and try to come to terms with what has happened to you. It will not be easy, but we must all soldier on.'

* * *

The letter box rattled and a small blue envelope fluttered down to the doormat.

163

Rose Meadows picked it up and-frowned. It was postmarked London, but she did not recognize the handwriting. Every day she hoped for some word from Lucy, but this was not the girl's spidery scrawl.

It was addressed to 'Mr and Mrs William Meadows, Hartscombe, Gloucestershire'. It's just as well that Hartscombe is a small place, where we all know each other, Rose thought, noting that there was no street address or any reference to the school. Well, she wasn't going to wait until her husband came home from school in order to satisfy her curiosity. It was addressed to both of them, so she was within her rights to open it.

Having read the letter she gave a squeal of delight and danced around the room with tears of joy running down her cheeks.

'I don't know if you remember me,' Jenny Adams had written, 'but I was Emma's roommate at St Bee's. I'm in London now, helping to train girls as VADs. Emma had let me know that

Lucy had left home and was believed to have come to London. I'm pleased to let you know that I've found Lucy here, in the very same hospital, where she is working as a maid. While no doubt you would wish her to be sent home at once, she has signed a contract to work here and cannot be released for another three months. In the meantime I know that you will be much relieved to know that she is safe and well. I shall keep an eye on her as much as I can.'

Rose thought of her husband, busy in his classroom, trying to keep the worry from showing on his face. Why should he be made to wait a minute longer to hear that his youngest child was safe and well? Without another thought she flew across the playground, with Towser at her heels. She burst into his classroom without bothering to knock.

'Rose! Can't you see we're in the middle of a lesson here?'

'It's Lucy!' she cried, waving the letter. 'She's all right!'

Aware of the interested glances from

the children assembled here, she smiled at them and left the room. There would be time enough later to discuss this most happy outcome, and to decide what they should do next.

When he came in for his lunch, Rose could see that the lines of worry on her husband's face had been smoothed out. 'When did this come, Rose?'

'In the first post this morning, of course. You don't think I'd keep it from you a moment longer than necessary, do you? Isn't it wonderful, Will? Lucy is quite safe, and Emma's friend will keep an eye on her.'

'It's good news that the girl is all right, of course it is. But working as a maid? Scrubbing floors, and probably scouring pans covered in all sorts of germs? If that's what she chooses to do with her life she can come home and take on the tasks which Cherry used to do, and I shall tell her so!'

'Of course you'll go to London and fetch her home, won't you, Will?'

'I'll do no such thing. As you can see

from this letter, the girl has signed a contract, and she must honour that.'

'Then we must at least send her the money for her train fare home when she's free from her obligations.'

Will held up a hand as if he was directing traffic. 'I have no intention of mollycoddling the girl, my dear. Presumably she's receiving some sort of wage at this place, however small that may be. Let her save it up and pay her own way home.'

'But oh, Will! Is that wise? She has run away once. What if she decides to do that again, and ends up where we'll never find her?'

'I think you'll find she'll be glad to come home again, after having had a taste of life in the outside world. She'll appreciate everything you do for her all the more after having had to earn her own living in London. A maid! Just think of it. No more lying in bed until the last minute and galloping into school seconds before the last bell. Young Miss Lucy will be rising at five o'clock and starting work before the sun is up. That is something I never thought I'd live to see.'

Unable to settle down to housework after receiving such marvellous news, Rose sat down to write to Pierce. She wrote a weekly letter, sent to him because he couldn't get out of bed, but addressed to Emma as well. She expected her two elder children would view Lucy's escapade in different ways. Pierce would chuckle over it, seeing it in the light of his own adventures. Emma, on the other hand, would understand just how frantic with worry their mother had been. Having been out in the world for the past three years she would be aware of the dangers that awaited young girls alone in a strange city, and she would be able to share her parents' relief that Lucy was safe.

During the early days of her nursing training Emma had performed her share of menial tasks. She, more than any of them, would understand what Lucy was going through now. Rose suspected that Emma would say it served her right.

However, Emma wasn't thinking of Lucy now. In fact she was not even aware that the girl had been found. Jenny had dashed off a note to let her know of this, but Emma hadn't received it. Even now it was languishing in her pigeon hole in the entrance hall of the Nurses' Home.

Emma was on her way to France, determined to find out what had happened to James Townsend. The channel crossing was rough and, as the ship pitched and tossed, she sat on the deck, surrounded by nurses, soldiers and officers, all on their way to the war torn country.

Was she mad? James was dead, so what did she hope to achieve by coming to a battlefield? Would he even have an identifiable grave she could visit? It would have been far better to have waited until the war was over, when she could have visited some neat cemetery, in company with other grieving wives and sweethearts.

She only knew that she had to speak to those who had served with him, possibly someone who had seen him die. She could not rest until she had in some small way shared his last moments.

For her journey to France Emma had linked up with a group of First Aid Nursing Yeomanry women, Fanys, as they were known. Such women served in a variety of ways, not only helping wounded men but also driving ambulances and running soup kitchens and canteens. They also provided a mobile bath unit which carried ten collapsible baths. Mud covered, often lice-ridden, men were thus offered the luxury of a bath, which must have done a great deal for their morale. These women were not only courageous but immensely useful as well.

Emma was readily accepted by those she had met because of her nursing background. She knew that her uniform would be a passport to acceptance wherever she went, but here she had the added privilege of being able to find transport. Most of the Fanys held driving licences, and some were able mechanics as well. Women in England might not have won the right to vote yet, but here, in the man's world of war, they moved about with ease and confidence.

Emma's new friend, Mary Willis, walked unsteadily across the deck and came to sit beside her.

'You won't be able to go directly to find that field hospital where your young man was working, you know, but we'll do our best to pass you from one place to another.'

'I understand that. And if I can give a hand here and there along the way, I'll be more than willing.'

'If that's the case, I don't know why you don't apply to work over here permanently. They can always use more trained nurses. The VADs do sterling work, but some things are a bit beyond them.'

'Unfortunately, I only have ten days' leave and then I have to go back. I promised Matron I'd stay at St Bee's for another year and I can't let her down, especially when she's been so understanding.'

'Your young man was a doctor at your hospital before he volunteered?'

'Exactly, but despite the fact that the need here is so great, nurses are needed on the home front as well, you know. People don't stop getting ill because there's a war on.'

'What is it that you hope to achieve by coming to France?'

Emma shrugged. 'I don't really know. I suppose I shan't really accept that he's gone until I speak to those who were with him when he died. Oh, I'm sure his mother will get a letter from someone in authority eventually, but nobody will notify me because I'm not listed as his next of kin.'

'Won't his mother contact you?'

'I doubt she even knows about me. We weren't officially engaged, you see, and I don't know if he's told her about us. There wasn't time for him to go home to see his parents before he left England. Anyway, those letters are all the same, aren't they? Your son, husband, brother died instantly and would have felt no pain. I've been shown a lot of those letters by patients at our hospital, and they all seem to be the same.'

'Aren't you being a bit cynical?' Mary asked.

'Am I? I don't think so. People need to grasp at what little comfort they can find and naturally they want to believe that their loved ones didn't suffer. As for me, I know I'm setting out on a wild goose chase, but even if I don't find anyone who worked with James, at least I'd have tried to do something. In later years I'll have that to look back on.'

When the ship docked at Calais, Emma was stunned by the sight that met her eyes. There were uniformed men everywhere, wearing the insignia of regiments not only from Britain, but from Canada and Australia as well.

Some of them, who were probably going on leave, were lining up to board the ship from which she was about to disembark. Others were lying on stretchers, blood-soaked bandages showing that they were waiting for a hospital ship to take them back to England. There were nurses everywhere, offering comfort where they could. Emma felt the urge to roll up her sleeves and join them, but she had to follow her new friends to their billet.

The next few days passed in a blur as she was taken from one place to another with the Fanys, wherever they happened to be going. Very often after arriving at a casualty clearing station or field hospital she would pitch in where she could, later to fall into an exhausted sleep in some draughty tent or a corner in what had once been some stately home. The next morning she'd be off again, sometimes taking a totally different direction.

After days of this aimless wandering

she was almost in despair. How foolish she had been to start on this with no fixed plan! Searching for James in this ruined landscape was like looking for a needle in a haystack, except that the word conjured up good clean hay in a peaceful country farm, not this nightmare of ruined houses and broken fences. Of course she was not allowed anywhere near the trenches, where desperate men fought for survival every hour of the day. The wounded ones she saw in the field hospitals assured her that hell could be no worse than what they encountered there.

Everywhere she went she asked everyone she met whether they knew of Dr James Townsend. Each time she met with denials. There were just too many makeshift hospitals, too many doctors. Finally she found someone who had known him, but what she heard brought her no peace.

She was helping to feed a soldier whose hands were swathed in bandages, when a man in the next bed overheard what she was telling him.

'Cor, don't I wish my girl would come looking for me!' he said. 'Is it Doctor James Townsend you're talking about?'

'Yes, that's right. Have you heard of him?'

'Treated me in the hospital, he did. Of course, it was just the collywobbles I had back then. Now I've got my foot shot off, so it's back home for me, and I won't pretend I'm sorry.'

'When was that? I mean, did he look after your foot?'

'Nah. We both got blown up together. I was a stretcher bearer, see, and me and this other chap, we was coming back carrying a casualty when this shell hit the hospital tent. I got this packet and my mate got blown to pieces, along with everybody in that blessed tent. Doctor Townsend, he was standing there in the entrance, waiting for us. He didn't stand a chance.'

'I see.' Well, she had got what she had come for, hadn't she? Here was someone who had actually witnessed James's death. And there probably wasn't a grave she could visit, because there hadn't been any remains to bury. A tear ran down her cheek and she brushed it away angrily.

'Sorry, Miss! I forgot you was his missus-to-be. What'll you do now, then? Go back home, I suppose.'

Emma nodded. There was no point in staying on. She would volunteer to go back on the hospital ship. She could do some good there.

11

The following morning, having reported to the Sister in charge of the VADs who were to accompany the wounded back to England, she began the slow job of helping to settle the patients on board. Returning to the dock after leaving one particularly ill man below decks, she noticed a fleet of ambulances coming in. These vehicles disgorged many more men, all in various stages of distress.

'Mind where you're going, man!' she heard a voice roar, as a porter came charging round the corner, pushing a laden trolley and narrowly missed several of the wounded who were hobbling along on sticks.

Emma knew that voice. Frozen to the spot, she watched as the speaker turned around to face the ship. 'James,' she whispered, and then everything went blank.

'Give her some air!'

She came back to the present to find herself lying on a stretcher near the water's edge. Gulls were wheeling and crying overhead and for a moment she wondered if she was a child again, going on a promised seaside holiday, although she had never actually experienced one.

Then James's voice reached her. 'Go about your business everyone. I'll see to this young woman. She's my fiancée, and she's not hurt. I believe she's just had a little fainting spell.'

'James! I've found you! You're alive!'

'And it appears that I've found you, although what you're doing here I can't imagine. I must say it's made my day, though. But why did you pass out? Haven't you had any breakfast?'

'It was the shock of seeing you,' Emma explained, struggling to sit up. 'Everyone thought you were dead. Your name was in the casualty lists in all the newspapers last week. Only yesterday I met a soldier who told me he'd seen you killed. He received his own wounds in the same attack.'

'Ah! I think I know what must have happened. There was another doctor, you see — a Jim Townsend, a Canadian. I met him once. I heard that he'd bought it recently, up near the front lines. When the report went in somebody must have got the two of us confused. Honestly, Emma, it's such chaos back there it's a wonder there aren't far more muddles of that sort.'

'But it wasn't you! It wasn't you,' Emma wept.

'Never mind all that now, James said, kissing her lightly on the forehead. 'You're here now and we must do something to celebrate. First, though, I must send a marconigram to let my parents know I'm alive and well. They're sure to have spotted my name in the casualty lists, and Mother must be in a dreadful state.'

★   ★   ★

Emma spent the night in cramped quarters with several other nurses in what had once been a storage shed for grain. It was a dusty place that affected her lungs, and at times she found it hard to breathe. After the excitement of the day she was unable to drop off to sleep in any case, so she spent the night half propped up against someone's kit bag, sure that she'd look like the witch of Endor in the morning.

James had promised her that he'd come for her in the morning and they'd spend the day together.

'Can you do that? I mean, surely the wounded don't stop coming in, do they? I haven't heard the guns stop since I got here. In fact, I could hear them when we were on the way over in the boat.'

'We do get days off, you know. If we didn't, we'd never be able to carry on. As it is, we're on our feet for hours on end, sometimes without even a meal break. I'll find someone to change places with me. After all, I've come back from the dead, haven't I? I deserve some consideration.'

'Doctor Lazarus,' she teased him.

True to his word, James came for her early in the morning. 'I've managed to swing it,' he told her. 'I'm off duty for three whole days.'

'So what's in store for me today, James? A quick tour of the trenches?'

He suddenly looked more serious than she had ever seen him. 'Will you marry me, Emma?'

'Of course I will. Just as soon as this rotten war is over, we'll have the wedding to end all weddings.'

'Actually, I was thinking of today.'

'What? Do you mean our engagement starts now?'

'No. I mean let's get married here and now. I've spoken to the chaplain, and he'll be happy to oblige. He said it'll make a nice difference from all the nasty things he usually has to do.'

Emma didn't need to ask what those tasks might be — she could already guess. 'Oh, darling, I wish we could, but it's impossible,' she said sadly.

'I don't agree, unless you insist upon being married in white satin, with orange blossoms in your hair.'

'We mustn't forget our parents. They'll want to see us married.'

'I'm sure they will, but we'll do it all again after the war, and invite everyone we know to attend.'

'Then there's Matron.'

'Invite her, too.'

'That's not what I mean, silly. I am committed to staying on here at St Bee's, and you know full well that married women aren't allowed to nurse.'

'Matron doesn't have to know. In any case, I don't know why a married woman can't carry on working if she's childless and her husband is away, serving in the war.'

Emma continued to raise objections, each one weaker than the next, and James continued to shoot them down. At last he pulled her to her feet and said 'I've saved the best until last. I'll take you to Paris for our honeymoon.'

'Now you are being silly! Paris, in the middle of a war!'

'It's not silly at all. Lots of people go there on short leave. I've a lorry all lined up, so if you've no more excuses, miss, I'll run and alert the chaplain. And before you say you don't have a ring, I have one here in my pocket.'

'Where on earth did you get that?'

'I bought it in Gloucester, before I left. I meant to ask you then but I lost my nerve. I've carried it next to my heart ever since. Now listen, Emma, this is serious. Do you want to marry me now, or not? I really don't want to go to Paris on my own.'

'Of course I'll marry you!' she told him, unable to hold back the smile which spread all over her face.

'Right, then. No time to seal it with a kiss. I must dash and get hold of the padre before he leaves.'

Many thoughts went through Emma's head as she waited for James to return. What about Mum and Dad? They'd be so disappointed at missing this day and she hoped they wouldn't be too cross. But James was alive after all and she loved him with all her heart. Life in wartime was so uncertain, and she couldn't bear the thought of losing him again, without really having known him at all.

Soon they were standing in front of the little clergyman, attended by a colleague of James and that young man's best girl, who was a nurse.

Emma was wearing nurse's uniform instead of a white gown and when they emerged from the little room after they were made man and wife it was to the sound of guns booming rather than church bells pealing. Still, without a doubt, it was the happiest day of her life.

Hours later, as they strolled hand in hand beside the Seine, she felt that her heart might burst from happiness. As they talked of the future, of where they would live and the children they might have, she knew that she would love James forever. Her husband! She could hardly believe it.

When a boy on a bicycle delivered a marconigram to Rose Meadows, she wasn't unduly upset. For most people who received one from France, such an envelope augured bad news, but since the family had no one at the front, she assumed that it must have come to them by mistake.

She had to read the contents of the missive three times over before she could take it in. *Married this morning. Letter to follow. Love from Emma and James Townsend.*

She rushed outside and thrust the paper under her husband's nose. He was pruning her rose bushes and gave a cry of dismay as a thorn pierced his skin. 'Look out, Rose! See what you made me do.'

'Never mind that, Will. Just read this, will you?'

He snatched the paper from her. 'Who on earth are the Townsends? Never heard of them.'

'Don't be such a fool, darling!

It means we have a doctor for a son in law. And about time, too! But I can't think why they didn't invite us to come to Gloucester, can you? I suppose it has something to do with him popping off to the war. Oh well, never mind. I expect we'll hear all about it when she comes home.'

THE END

We do hope that you have enjoyed reading this large print book.

Did you know that all of our titles are available for purchase?

We publish a wide range of high quality large print books including:
Romances, Mysteries, Classics
General Fiction
Non Fiction and Westerns

Special interest titles available in large print are:
The Little Oxford Dictionary
Music Book, Song Book
Hymn Book, Service Book

Also available from us courtesy of Oxford University Press:
Young Readers' Dictionary
(large print edition)
Young Readers' Thesaurus
(large print edition)

For further information or a free brochure, please contact us at:
Ulverscroft Large Print Books Ltd.,
The Green, Bradgate Road, Anstey,
Leicester, LE7 7FU, England.
Tel: (00 44) **0116 236 4325**
Fax: (00 44) **0116 234 0205**

Other titles in the
Linford Romance Library:

TRUTH, LOVE AND LIES

Valerie Holmes

Florence Swan's plan is to escape from Benford Mill School for young women before she is forced to work in their cotton mill. Naïve, ambitious and foolhardy, she ventures out on her own, her path crossing that of Mr Luke Stainbridge — a man accused of being mad. He has returned home from imprisonment in France to discover that his home has been claimed by an imposter. Together they find the truth, disproving clever lies, and discover life anew.

BITTERSWEET DECEPTION

Liz Fielding

Kate Thornley's catering business was suffering, so she unhesitatingly accepted the offer of a contract to set up a tearoom in the grounds of a stately home. However, if she'd known that media mogul Jason Warwick was to be her boss she would have turned it down flat. His devastating good looks ensured constant female attention. Kate wasn't interested in a temporary affair — and that was all he was offering. But could she defend herself against his seductive charm?

RETURN TO BUTTERFLY ISLAND

Rikki Sharp

After thirty years' absence, China Stuart returns to her birth place, the remote island of West Uist, to attend her aunt Beatrice's funeral — and finds she has inherited Stuart Grange. As if the funeral isn't traumatic enough, James McKriven, a land developer, is claiming the rights to China's ancestral home. Amongst the cobwebs and the cracked ceilings, China finds love, but faces the ghosts of the past . . . and the reason her family fled the island all those years ago.

A COLLECTOR OF HEARTS

Sally Quilford

It's 1936. Level-headed Caroline Conrad does not believe in ghosts, but even she is shaken when strange things start happening at a Halloween House Party. At Stony Grange Abbey, the atmosphere certainly unsettles her, but the presence of the handsome, albeit changeable, Blake Laurenson increases her sense of unease. Then Caroline finds herself fighting to clear her name. She's accused of stealing the priceless Cariastan Heart — has Blake framed her? And just who is the mysterious Prince Henri?

MEMORIES OF LOVE

Margaret Mounsdon

When Emily Sinclair discovers that deckchair attendant James Bradshaw is two-timing her with Madame Zora, she sprays the details in brilliant pink paint outside the fortune-teller's caravan. It's six years before Emily sees James again and she realises that she still loves him. The only trouble is, James has purchased the Victorian play house theatre she manages and, unless she can turn its fortune around, he is threatening to close it down.

SHADOWMAN

Della Galton

Karen and Rob's show-jumping yard is in financial difficulties. And so is their marriage. Then someone starts sending nasty, anonymous letters. They seem to have an enemy who is determined to wreck their lives, but who? Is it a vindictive stranger or could it be someone closer to home . . . ? Karen is determined to find out before she loses everything she loves.